SHAR'S STORY

BOOKMAIL EPISODES

LEYA LAYNE

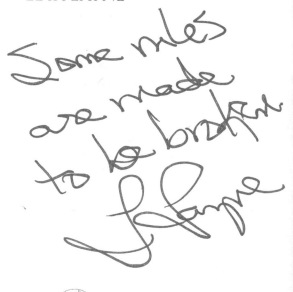

Some rules
are made
to be broken

[signature]

Trigger Warnings

While this book is meant to be a quick, fun romance with lots of spice, there
are discussions of topics that could be triggering for readers. To be respectful
to those who need warnings and those who see them as spoilers, I have placed
the trigger warnings on my website. Scan this code to check the site.

This is a work of fiction. Names, characters, places, and incidents are products
of the author's imagination or are used fictitiously and are not to be construed
as real. Any resemblance to actual events, locals, organizations, or persons,
living or dead, is entirely confidential.

No portion of this book may be reproduced in any form without written
permission from the publisher or author, except as permitted by U.S.
copyright law.

ACKNOWLEDGMENTS

This one is dedicated to my ARC readers for You've Got Bookmail who asked for Shar's full story. If not for you, this book would not have existed.

I also want to acknowledge the Roberts Row and Friends May 25th Crew. Somewhere back in February, we decided to release novels on the same date. It was that delusional decision that allowed Shar's Story to come to life in 2024 instead of being pushed back to a later date.

CHAPTER 2
SHAR

Hair and makeup never took very long. She was blessed with near flawless skin, and her dark blonde hair was to the middle of her back, thick and wavy. Of course, she hadn't always been this woman everyone clamored to have in their ads. She was an awkward, gangly kid, even in her early teens. Puberty kicked in later for her, but when it did, it put curves in all the right places. Though she'd never been a runway model at barely 5 foot 7 inches, she looked great in photos and on video. Something about growing up in the south made her a natural actress, able to show all kinds of emotions at the drop of a hat.

"Shar, darling," Jacques, the photographer, called to her as soon as she stepped from the tent.

"Good morning, my friend. Are you ready to make me gorgeous?"

"The camera only captures what exists, and you, my dear, are perfection."

Shar smiled. Their initial exchanges were always the same, full of pandering and platitudes, as was expected. Still, she liked working with him. He knew how to pull out her best angles, capitalize on her strengths, and give the client exactly what they were paying her for, a flawless ad. All that, and he went out of his way to make her feel good about herself. Not that she was ever down on herself. On the contrary, her confidence was a brick wall, protecting her from anything the media might say about her being a little bottom heavy or getting up there in age. At 26, she knew she was on the tail end of a career in the industry and would soon be relegated to anti-aging make up and skin care ads, or, heaven forbid, travel brochures.

Speaking of travel, the client brought her out to this gorgeous backdrop, only to dress her up like an unlikely tourist. Her makeup toned down the natural glow of her tanned skin, and they put her in a short, bobbed wig.

"So, what's the scenario?" she asked, after following Jacques to the edge of the camp where, presumably, she'd be posing.

Jacques looked up with a gleam in his eye that made the hair on her neck stand up. She looked around for Jerry, about to ask him what in the world was going on, when a distinguished, older gentleman stepped out of the tent furthest from hers. By older, she'd say late 30s, early 40s. He was attractive, with salt and pepper at his temples and perfectly coifed, nearly black hair at the top. He was in dark blue dress slacks and a white button-down with the sleeves rolled to just below his elbows. His forearms were perfectly formed, and warmth spread through Shar's middle. She didn't usually get with older men because they tended to have more expectations, but this man could get it.

Jacques cleared his throat loudly. "I thought you'd like the eye candy. I know I could photograph that all night long!"

"That means nothing," Shar said with a shake of her head. "You're so attached to that lens, you'd photograph a speck of dirt all night long."

They were both laughing when the handsome stranger walked their way. At the same time, Jerry made an appearance.

"Where have you been?" Shar asked him, and he smirked.

"I have been doing my job, madame," he said with a flourished bow. She lifted her brow. "Making you rich and famous."

He bumped his hip against hers and scurried off to where Jacques was setting up the equipment. Jerry's behavior was so unexpected that she stood frozen in place wondering what just happened. She was about to follow him and ask for specifics when a shadow blocked her from the sun. She looked up and into a gorgeous pair of crystal blue eyes. She couldn't tell the color when he first left his tent, but damn if those eyes wouldn't forever be branded into her memory now.

"You must be Sharlene Maxwell," he said with an accent Shar couldn't quite place.

"Shar is fine. And you are?"

"Very pleased to meet you, petit chaton."

Shar wasn't sure what he said, or even if his accent was authentic. She also didn't care. Plenty of people came into this industry trying to reinvent themselves into something, someone, different from whom they'd always been. She even considered creating a new life story for herself, but it seemed like too much work to try and maintain. Besides, her story was what brought her to this point in her life and career. Her ability to not only survive but thrive was something to celebrate not hide.

Shar raised a brow at the man standing before her. "But do you have a name?"

He blinked once, like he was trying to recall his next move in the game he was playing. "Yes, of course. My name is Henri Durand."

"Wonderful. Shall we get to work, Henri?"

He nodded and held out his arm for her to hold, and they walked toward the cliff's edge.

7

The shoot ended right at dusk. The photos were meant to chronicle a Pretty Woman or Ugly Betty homage of sorts where the handsome man sees her in her tourist attire and terrible wig. He watches her from a distance and is entranced by her movements. The energy she exudes doesn't match the facade she shows, and in the end, she sheds the mask to reveal the woman beneath. Shar wasn't sure what this story had to do with selling watches, but her job was to look pretty, not to master in marketing. Hell, that's why she hired Jerry to do her own marketing.

"I'll meet you for dinner at your hotel, gorgeous," Jerry said as he walked her to where Thomas stood waiting with the door of the SUV open for her.

"Don't keep me waiting, Jerry. I know you have some news, and I hate you've made me wait half the day already."

"It'll be worth the wait. I promise," he said with a wink.

When they turned onto the main road, Thomas broke the silence. "You looked like you were having a ball out there, really in your element."

Shar's eyes opened from where she'd been relaxing against the headrest, and she smiled at him. "I love my job, Thomas. It's like getting to reinvent myself every day, and yet I still get to stay Sharlene."

"That makes sense. Work isn't a chore when you love what you do. At least that's what my mother always said. Then she'd tell me to do my chores." He chuckled at his own joke, and Shar had to hold back a snort.

"Do you love what you do now, Thomas?"

"Yes, ma'am. I've met lots of people and seen lots of things I might not have ever seen without this job. In case you can't tell, I'm not from around here, so this job lets me live like I'm from here and yet play tourist every day. It's a great time."

"Makes total sense," she said and leaned her head back, closing her eyes again.

Thankfully, he let the conversation end. Whenever she finished a shoot, she liked to mentally unwind on the ride back to her hotel. When given a choice, she opted for a hotel that was at least thirty minutes from the location. The ride gave her time to mentally prepare beforehand and relax afterward. This ride, however, wasn't as relaxing as it could have been. Her mind continuously wandered back to Jerry's cryptic behavior.

"He better be at the hotel when I get there," she muttered to herself, nostrils flaring in annoyance.

When Jerry greeted her at the curb, he must have perceived her surprise. "You didn't think I'd be here, did you?"

"Don't make that face at me, Jerry. We both know you're very good at your job, but punctuality is not always your best attribute. You like to make me wait far too often."

"But I always make it worth it, unlike some of the dudes you date."

"Bastard! And for the record, I don't date. I fuck." She looked at him from the corner of her eye as they made their way inside to the hotel's four-star restaurant. "You're right, though. Not all of them were worth the trip to the room." She laughed when his eyes slid toward her, and he shook his head with a smirk.

Once they were seated and their drink orders placed, Shar folded her hands on the table and looked directly at Jerry. He regarded her for a long while before taking in a deep breath.

"How long have we known each other?" he asked.

Shar's eyes narrowed, eyeing him warily. "Why does it sound like you're breaking up with me? Have you gotten better clients? There's no way you're retiring." The look on Jerry's face was one of utter confusion, which caused Shar to stop the barrage of questions. "What's that look for?"

"What in the hell, Shar? Where did all of that come from?"

"You and your cryptic-assed behavior today since you disappeared during hair and makeup."

He chuckled. "I told you that I had something in the works and would tell you about it later, over dinner, and your first thought was that I was quitting you? You're my damn meal ticket, not to mention my bestie. Besides, I think Geoffrey would leave me if we broke up. He wouldn't be able to handle my inconsolable ass."

Trying to hold back her laughter, Shar snorted, which only made Jerry laugh harder. Within seconds, all eyes were on them. The collective disgust at their display made Shar laugh harder.

"I'm so glad we actually enjoy each other's company, my friend. I'd hate it if we had to pretend to be cordial in silence and whispered pretense," she said loudly enough to be heard by the nearest tables.

Jerry stifled another laugh and then grew serious. "You do know that you are nearly at the point in your career where people will recognize you. We probably don't want to offend the uppity and crotchety."

Shar raised a brow. "Since when do you care?"

"Since I am working on the biggest contract either of us have seen," he whispered like they were a couple of co-conspirators about to take over the world.

"Do tell."

Jerry leaned in close. "I'm in negotiations with Velocity Communications."

"Velocity!" Shar yelled in excitement, garnering more looks and turned up noses.

Jerry held his finger to his mouth. "Nothing is finalized yet. It might not happen, but if it does, it's going to be big. Multiple ad campaigns, photo and video, lots of travel."

Shar's eyes widened. This might be her one chance to

really make a name for herself. Velocity had recently released their first-generation phones, and they were dominating the market in satellite WIFI. She didn't have any experience with their products, but she'd heard talk about them becoming the next big thing in telecommunications. Yes, this could be her big break.

CHAPTER 3
MACK

"Good morning, Mr. Mackenzie."

"Good morning, Janet," Mack said, never breaking stride toward his office.

No matter how many times he'd asked the woman to call him Mack, she wouldn't. Hearing 'Mr. Mackenzie' always put him on edge, looking around for his father. That man had been long gone, but the visceral response still happened, and he hated it. Jaw clenched, he yelled back down the corridor for her to send Kevin to his office.

Kevin, his partner and marketing genius, had been the backbone of the company since day one. It didn't hurt that he had also been one of Mack's best friends since high school. They knew each other so well that it felt as if Kevin could visualize everything Mack wanted before the words were fully out to describe it. In order to break through the wall the big cellular companies had built, Velocity Communications would have to get the average consumer to reimagine themselves as more than just a cellular user.

"You wanted to see me, boss?" Kevin's voice came through the wide, oak door before his body.

"It's about time," Mack quipped from across the huge mahogany desk.

Everything in his office was scaled to match the expanse of the room and the wall-to-ceiling windows that looked out over the harbor. When he met with the designers to create this space, he'd been very specific that he wanted real wood. He wanted the room to convey lasting strength. Though sleek, modern, and metal seemed to be the direction everyone else was going for nowadays, Mack wanted to give the impression of tried, tested, and trustworthy. Thus, the room resembled an old, comfortable study more than a corporate office with its worn, leather couch, built-in bookshelves, and faux fireplace.

Kevin laughed as he took a seat across the desk and rested his foot on his knee. "You do know it's 8:05 in the morning, right?"

"And you know that I have been up since five."

"No wonder you're always looking so damn tired."

Mack narrowed his eyes before quipping. "If I look tired it's because I'm trying to do my job and yours too. Why am I up at 5 a.m. coming up with marketing ideas rather than seeing a proposal on my desk?"

"Why in the hell are you up at 5 a.m. period, unless you have some warm and soft company? No one should be up at that god awful hour!"

Cracking a smile, Mack agreed. "I can't stop worrying about this new release, man. We have to do something big. When we put out the prototype, we got some interest, but it feels like Version One just fell flat."

They had built the company from the ground up to become one of the biggest names in WIFI and satellite service along the entire east coast, but breaking into the cellular arena was proving much more difficult.

"Right," Kevin said in agreement. "We're going to have to work this a little differently from how we've approached our services. We're not only offering coverage, we're promising a product when people already have products they trust that work with our services. They don't like change."

"No, they don't." Mack walked around the desk. "But they like luxury. We need to make them feel like they're getting luxury for pennies. But how?" He paced.

Kevin fidgeted with his phone, and Mack smiled seeing that it was their Version Two, set to release later this year. When Kevin looked up, Mack pointed to the device and asked how he liked it.

"Dude, it's awesome! You know I'm a gadget guy, so I've had a lot of different phones in my life. This is the first that has truly felt like a computer in my hand. I just sent you some of my ideas. If you want, I can project them onto the big screen."

Mack nodded and went back to his desk, pressing the button to drop down the screen that covered most of the bookshelves along the wall. Another button, and the projector clicked on. Kevin tapped on his phone a few times, and images appeared on the screen. They spent the next two hours tossing ideas back and forth before they were both satisfied with the overall plan.

"Now, we just need to find the right face," Mack mused.

"You've always been the face of the company."

"Yes, but this is much bigger than just our services, and we need to appeal to a wider market. We need a woman who can portray multiple facets of life, carefree traveler, corporate businesswoman, homemaker, rich and glamorous, you know."

"I got you, and I have some ideas of who already."

Mack's eyes lit up. "You already know someone who can check off all those boxes?"

"Of course. You know I've been watching the up-and-coming faces. Want to see who I have in mind?"

"Nah, I trust you. I have to get ready for my trip anyway."

Other than the surfing, Mack wasn't looking forward to traveling to California. He was an east-coast boy through and through, and he hated the idea of being out there during an earthquake. Unfortunately, most of their investors lived on the west coast, and he had to give a report on their returns. Thankfully, he only had to make this trip twice a year, and he always tacked on a couple extra days to relax. He was going to do his best this time to actually relax because the next few months would be nonstop.

"Hey, good luck with the investors."

Mack waved his hand. "They should be fine. We've all made money this quarter, and this new direction will broaden our reach even further."

He didn't feel quite as confident as his words portrayed considering the lackluster response to the Version One, but he was going to sell the hell out of Version Two with Kevin's marketing plan. As Mack leaned back in his chair, deep in thought, Kevin stood to leave, breaking his concentration.

"Oh yeah, Kev, make sure you get a guy too. I may pop into some of the ads, but I'll be busy selling this thing. We'll also need some teens, but those will be separate individual ads."

"Gotcha!"

Swiveling his chair around, Mack turned to face the harbor. This was either going to be the biggest thing he'd ever accomplished, or it was all going to blow up in his face. Either way, it was time to get things moving. First, though, he needed to release some tension. Picking up his Version One, he sent a text to the number he knew would get a quick response.

Mona and her portable massage table floated into his foyer. The way she carried that thing around was magical. With her 5 ft 3 in, lithe frame, it was a miracle she could even pick it up high enough to carry it up the stairs, but here she was, right on time.

"Sloan, darling. It's been a while," Mona said after setting the table on the floor and reaching out to pull him close enough to kiss his cheeks.

He bristled at the use of his first name. Mona was one of the few people he knew personally who insisted on calling him Sloan rather than Mack, no matter how many times he'd insisted otherwise. If he wasn't in desperate need of her services, he'd have sent her packing. Instead, he plastered on a smile.

"I'm so glad you could fit me in last minute. I have a flight later this afternoon, but I hate getting on a plane with my muscles this tense."

"I know just what you need," she purred, opening the table to set it up in the entryway. "We don't have a lot of time, so strip."

"Mona," he said through gritted teeth.

"The clock is ticking." She raised an eyebrow at him as she unfolded a sheet and covered the table. "Unless you're going to climb up here fully dressed."

"Keep goading me..." He stepped in close, pressing her up against the table's edge. "...and this table won't be the only thing I'm climbing onto."

Mona reached up to brush his hair back from where he had run his hands through it earlier. "I told you already, I know what you need. Now, are you going to let me relax you or what?"

Looking down into her eyes, his erection pressing into her abdomen, Mack made the decision to listen to his better sense and step back. He peeled off his shirt and let his pants fall to the floor. With a wink at Mona, who was eyeing the imprint on his boxer briefs, he climbed onto the table face down.

Mona dribbled oil down his spine and began working it into this skin, pressing into the muscles. Making her way from his waistband back up to his shoulders, the heel of her palm ran over a tight knot, and he winced. In true sadistic form, Mona pressed her palm repeatedly into the spot, trying to loosen the knot. When that didn't work, she attempted a different tactic, sliding her thumbs alongside each other and then in circular motions. Finally, she dug her elbow into the muscle until he moaned at the release. The pattern repeated along his other side until all the knots in his shoulders and back had been released.

He was so relaxed, that when she told him to flip over onto his back, he nearly jumped off the bed. Mona giggled, and Mack groaned, but he followed her directions. His erection had gone down while she tortured his back into submission. The moment she rubbed oil across his nipples, though, his dick sprang back to life. She knew just how sensitive his nipples were, and she teased them with each swipe of his chest. When her hands scrubbed down across his abs, as if she were washing clothes, he slid his hand up the back of her thigh, underneath the hem of her short shorts.

She looked over her shoulder at him and pursed her lips. "No touching." He pouted, pushing his bottom lip out. "Let me do my job, the job you're paying me for."

The way her hands were working into his waistband and then up under the hem of his briefs had him so hard that he nearly moaned out a promise to pay more, but he stopped himself. First, he had never had to pay for it, and he would not ruin their decades long friendship with such a disrespectful proposition. Mona had always made it clear that she accepted their casual situation as it was but that she was always open for more should he want it. That would never happen. They'd known each other far too long, and their similar dominant natures were not compatible for anything more than this.

When her fingers latched onto the waistband of his briefs, he lifted his hips, allowing her to slip them down and free his cock, which sprung upright. She chuckled, and he gave her a sheepish grin.

"Now that work is done, it's time to play," she announced, wrapping her fingers around his shaft.

"Let the games begin," he responded, and it was the last complete sentence either of them uttered.

Standing in the shower, hot water falling over his head and running down his body, Mack felt relaxed for the first time in over a week. His body was sated, his muscles loose, and his mind empty. It felt so good to just be, even if it would only last for a moment. As soon as he was packed and on the plane, he would tense up again in preparation for the meetings. But for this brief, beautiful moment, all was right with the world.

CHAPTER 4
MACK

The best part of flying to the west coast was gaining daytime hours. With the time change just passing, they were finally starting to get more daylight in the evenings, but it was nice to leave mid-afternoon and arrive with enough time to dip his head in the Pacific before nightfall. Within thirty minutes of getting to the hotel, he had a wetsuit on and a board in hand.

"Good evening, Mr. Mackenzie," the concierge called to him as he made his way out toward the beach exit.

"See you soon, Bruno. And it's Mack."

As soon as his toes hit the sand, he sprinted toward the surf. The sound of the ocean cracking against the shore called to him like a siren's song. His hair, fully released from its normally slicked back style, bounced wildly around his head. It was probably time for a haircut, but he didn't care. If not for the corporate expectations, he'd let his hair grow long until all the waves filled in, and he'd forego the daily suits and ties. In fact, he'd probably find a cabana on some tropical island and do nothing but surf and dive all day long. That wasn't his reality, though, so he'd enjoy the hell out of these moments when they came.

The beach between the hotel and the water was quiet with very few people lounging around. It was still early in the season, so it wasn't surprising for the hotel to have fewer occupants. Still, he tried to register the few people, as he breezed by them. One, in particular, caught his eye, nearly making him stumble. Her dark blonde hair shone in the setting sun. He didn't break his stride, but he found himself hoping she'd still be there when he came back in.

No sooner had that thought passed through his mind that he hit the waves and forgot everything except the smell, feel, and taste of salt water. Though he lived mere minutes from the Atlantic Ocean, he was always so busy that he rarely got the opportunity to get into the water. Hence why he was out here now, racing dusk, to wash away his cares. If he timed his rides right, he'd get maybe two good waves in before the sky darkened completely. Tomorrow, he'd spend most of the day in the surf before Wednesday's meetings with the investors. He needed this time to clear his head.

An hour later, he dragged himself and his board up on the sand, grateful for the physical exertion that would hopefully help him get a good night's sleep. As he stood catching his breath, Mack looked around for the woman he had seen earlier. She was there on the same chaise she had been lounging on when he first got into the water. Her head was tilted somewhat in his direction, but he couldn't see her eyes for the large, dark sunglasses she wore. He got the feeling it was her intention to hide her gaze from others, so she could view them freely. He didn't have it in him to approach her tonight, but he would look for her tomorrow. Picking up his board, he headed back inside for a hot shower, some quick room service, and a long sleep.

CHAPTER 5

SHAR

The day had been a total fiasco. Jerry booked her a couple of different gigs in Agua Pura, so she could have the opportunity to get in some beach time. Unfortunately, when she showed up at the venue for this afternoon's event, where she was supposed to be the MC, nothing was ready. The time had been changed without warning, so the 2 p.m. luncheon turned into a 4 p.m. happy hour. Rather than stay the full four hours they had booked her for, Shar left at the agreed upon 6 p.m. Since it was their mistake, and she had already gotten paid, she was not going to miss the last bit of daylight because of someone else's inability to plan ahead.

By the time she got to the hotel and changed, the sky was already a collage of pink, orange, and blue, leaning toward the arrival of dusk. It didn't matter. This evening was really to let the sound of the surf wash over her, seeping calm into her soul. She had been working nonstop, which was great for her bank account and her career, but her body and mind were struggling to keep up the pace. Since the sun was no longer directly overhead, she left her sunhat and caftan in the room and let her hair fall over her bare shoulders, framing her face and contrasting starkly with the bright yellow of her swimsuit. Without the tanning effects of the sun, there was no point in putting on her favorite bikini. Instead, she opted for a one-piece with cutouts on the side.

Most of the beach was empty, just how she was hoping it would be. Thanks to it being the dinner hour, everyone else was inside. She'd be just as happy to order something light from room service later. Her main gig for the week was paying the hotel anyway, including any incidentals, so she could take advantage of that service tonight without feeling like she was breaking the budget.

As she looked out over the surf, watching the ebb and flow of the ocean, a small grunt caught her attention. Without turning her head completely, she looked over to see a tall man with beautiful shoulders carrying a long surfboard. His dark blonde hair was disheveled and moving with the slight breeze. He stumbled while looking her way, and it was all she could do to stifle a laugh. She couldn't get a good look at his face, so she couldn't quite judge his age, but from the looks of that body, he was maybe in his late twenties at the most. A little young for her taste but good for a snack. She bit her lower lip when he walked toward the waves, that wetsuit doing everything for his perfectly formed ass.

Shar spent that next hour watching him bob up and down on the waves, holding her breath as he stood on the board. His body was toned and controlled, and he moved with the board like water ran through a stream, smoothly undulating his core to remain upright. She rubbed her thighs together. He was beautiful out there. As many times as she'd lain on the beach over the years, she had never paid attention to surfers before, but damn if he didn't have all her attention.

When he finally left the water and made his way back to the hotel, she let her eyes follow his path. Thankfully, her large sunglasses afforded her an open view of him without him being able to tell she was looking. Something in the tilt of his head, though, made her wonder if he didn't know. With nothing else to occupy her mind, she, too, headed back inside and up to her room. Maybe she'd catch him tomorrow.

What she had hoped would be a restful night was instead one full of titillating visions of a certain surfer. She imagined his hips moving between her legs in the same way they moved on that board last night. It was like he had surfed his way into her dreams, and when she woke up with the sun, there was an ache between her thighs. Not one to masturbate unless she couldn't sleep, Shar got up, scheduled a car, and decided on some retail therapy for the morning. She doubted her dream guy would be out on the water this early considering how late he was out last night.

Shar made her way onto the sand shortly after lunch. Her white bikini glowing in the midday sun. There were surprisingly few people out here. Not that she was complaining. Little ruins a quiet beach trip more than little ones kicking sand up everywhere or college kids nearly bowling everyone over while tossing balls back and forth. She loved coming early or late in the season when schools were still in session, and the likelihood of a busy summer beach was slim.

After smoothing shimmery lotion meant to highlight her naturally tanned skin all over, she spread her towel on the chaise. Though she would call herself a sun worshipper, she knew the importance of protecting her skin. Not only did the lotion contain a good SPF, but she also wore her floppy, white sunhat to further protect her face. That was the money maker, and she couldn't afford early wrinkles or weathered skin.

Movement in the water caught her eye, and she saw a

group bobbing up and down on boards out beyond the safe line marked for families with children. Instinctively, she knew he was out there before any of them made a move to stand on their boards. When they did, though, he immediately stood out from the crowd. She pulled her bottom lip between her teeth when she saw he was wearing nothing more than low-hung, board shorts, his strong shoulders and pecs clearly visible.

For the next couple hours, Shar lounged on the chaise with a fluffy romance novel in her hand watching him surf the waves. She brought the book because she thought the day would be boring without something spicy to stimulate her mind. Ok, maybe there was more she wanted stimulated than her mind, thus she had chosen a book with spice. He, however, was far more interesting than anything that lay on the page. He was real, close and wet. His long-line shorts clung to him in all the right places, and they sat low enough on his hips to show off that magic v. She reached into her tote bag for the folded fan she always carried with her. Wishing they were in a private villa or a secluded island, she waved the fan at her face, trying to cool the flush that had crept up her cheeks. At least no one could see the response other parts of her body were having.

When he finally made it safely to the shore, she watched his approach, willing him to look her way. All it would take was a smile, and she'd gladly drag him inside to her suite. When his eyes finally locked onto hers, heat crept further into her lower abdomen threatening to burn her from the inside out. Then he smiled, and her breath caught. It wasn't playful or even one given in greeting. With his teeth and dimples on full display, her gaze trailed up to his eyes, and the desire in them penetrated her to the core. Just then, a waiter leaned next to her offering a beverage menu. She went to wave him away but changed her mind.

"Did you notice the guy over there staring?"

The waiter looked up to see past her. "Surfer with wavy blonde hair plastered to his face?"

Shar looked over her shoulder to see him standing there like he was waiting for something. She turned back smiling.

"Yes. May I have a napkin and a pen, please? I'd like you to give him a message for me."

When she's finished the note, and the waiter walked off, Shar leaned back against the back of the chaise and looked out over the water. Suddenly, a song was playing through her mind, *Tonight's gonna be a good night. Tonight's gonna be a good, good night.*

CHAPTER 6

MACK

Mack continued looking toward the woman, the folded napkin in his hand long after the waiter had handed it to him. She never turned back again.

"Hey, Mack. We're gonna head to the bar. You coming?"

He unfolded the napkin and read the note.

Suite 316
7:30pm

Turning his attention from the woman to the young kid he'd been surfing with, he shook his head while walking in that direction. "Nah, man. You go ahead and enjoy. I'm gonna take this old body inside."

"Ok, bro. Nice hanging with you."

Mack nodded at the kid who was barely half his age and headed toward the elevator. Once inside, he looked back at the napkin and smiled. Presumptuous minx thought she was in charge. He would see how well she could take direction.

Before he could slip his keycard into the slot, his phone was ringing on the other side of the door. All he wanted was one day of peace and quiet, and maybe a good night to finish it off.

"Kevin, I hope you have good news."

"Sure do, boss."

Mack shook his head and moved into the bathroom to start the shower. He put the phone on speaker and started peeling off his wet swim trunks.

"Am I interrupting something?"

"No. I just got off the board and am about to jump in the shower to wash the salt off. Tell me what's got you calling me on my day of relaxation."

"Alright, real quick. We're in negotiations for one of the hottest mid-size models out there right now."

"Mid-size, huh?"

"You said we wanted someone that could speak to multiple demographics. When I say hot, she is hot. Want me to send you her portfolio?"

"Nope. I told you that I trust your judgment. What about a co-star for her?"

Mack reached into the shower to check the water temp and pressure. It was perfect.

"Not yet. No one really holds a candle to her. I'm still looking though. I might ask her agent if there's someone she has good chemistry with who might like to work on the campaigns with her."

"Ok, you do that. I'll get an update when I get back."

Mack didn't wait for Kevin to respond or even say goodbye. He just tapped the call end button and stepped into the stream, letting the warmth of the water run over his body. As much as he loved the rush when the cold, ocean water shocked his body, he equally loved the opposite transition of a hot shower afterward to relax the muscles he just worked the hell out of. While his body acclimated to the warmth, his mind turned to the woman he had left sitting outside. She was stunning, immediately catching his eye last night and then again this afternoon. The bright suits against her tanned skin were breathtaking and really drew attention to her curves. He wanted to get his hands on those hips and run them down her thick thighs.

There was something about a woman who was so comfortable in her skin that she was willing to show it off to everyone. He found himself hoping she'd still have on that bikini when he got to the room this evening. His dick got hard at the thought of untying those strings and letting it fall to the ground. Would she be just as comfortable when he had her naked in front of him, spread open like meal? He palmed himself as the water cascaded off the tip. The pressure of the water added to the sensation, and he fully grasped the shaft, working it up and down. Though it had barely been 36 hours since he'd had sex, he was already hard just thinking about her. That would not bode well for making sure she was satisfied, and he refused to embarrass himself in front of her. He sped up his strokes, squeezing on each movement until his balls tightened and his release had him leaning against the shower wall catching his breath.

At exactly 7:30, Mack was outside of her door. Part of him wanted to make her wait, but curiosity won out, and he knocked. She opened the door to the suite still dressed in her white, string bikini with coverup hanging off her shoulders. She took him in from the top of his head down to his bare feet. With no intention to impress her with Armani suits, he hadn't waste any time on his attire before coming to meet her.

"Hey," he said in as carefree a way as he could manage while drinking in the view of her tanned skin shining as beautifully in the artificial overhead light as it had in the sun. There was nothing subtle about this woman, and he was happy to appreciate it all.

"Hi, yourself," she responded. "Would you like to come in?"

"I'm not dressed to go anywhere else, and my plan is for you to not be dressed at all."

She smirked and stood just inside the open doorway, letting her coverup drop to the floor. He leaned against the jamb with his arm up, not bothering to close the door yet. She lifted her long blonde tresses from her neck and pulled the tie of her top loose. Holding those strings in the hand still holding her hair, she reached around her back with the other arm and pulled that tie loose as well. He raised a brow, and in one fluid motion, she released both her hair and the top, letting them fall.

He raked his gaze over her tits, and her nipples puckered under his scrutiny. His eyes narrowed with arousal, and she shivered under his gaze. When she grabbed the tie at her right hip, ready to bare it all, he stayed her hand with a shake of his head.

"No, leave those. I'll take care of them later."

The look on her face at his words, had him guessing those bottoms were already damp. He pushed off the door frame and stalked toward her, pushing the door closed with his foot. With his eyes trained on hers, he walked her backward toward the seating area without touching her. Her breaths came faster with each step.

"Lay on the couch," he said with an air of authority.

"Yes, sir."

He inwardly chuckled at her response and sat on the

armchair facing her. She was not submissive. He could easily tell that by her note on the napkin and the striptease in the open doorway, but she could learn. "Touch yourself," he said, gaze steady.

"Excuse me?"

"You heard me. Touch yourself. You've been thirsting over me since I first hit the sand this morning, so I know you're ready. Show me."

The truth was that he had no idea what time she'd come out to the beach. He hadn't seen her from the water. The fact she didn't argue told him it didn't matter because he was close enough to correct.

"And what will I get in return?"

He shook his head, eyes narrowing in faux disappointment, but he said nothing. Instead, he rose from the chair and walked toward the door.

"Wait, where are you going?"

He smiled and quickly schooled his expression. She didn't want him to leave. He doubted she really even wanted to question him. She just thought he was going to cater to her whims. That wasn't going to happen, at least not that easily. When he didn't stop walking, she ran to get in front of him before he could open the door.

"Look, I'm not sure what just happened, but you caught me off guard. I thought you were going to touch me." She swallowed visibly. "That we would touch each other." She reached out a hand toward his chest.

He looked down at her, and she gasped when his hand came up around her neck, holding her against the door. She stared at him wide-eyed and panting. He'd have placed bets that no one had ever manhandled her like this before. Though tears welled in the corners of her eyes at the pressure on her throat, her breathing and hooded expression spoke of arousal more than fear.

Keeping his voice low, his words came out more like a

snarl. "I'm not here to do your bidding, little girl, nor am I here to be questioned. If you listen, we can both get what we want." Her eyes widened. She was definitely turned on by this. "Are you ready to listen now, Pretty?" Without taking a second to think, she nodded, at least as much as she could with his hand still pinning her to the door by the throat. He reached up with his free hand and wiped the moisture from her eyes. "I believe you. Now, go do as I said."

She swallowed, and he released her. She immediately turned around and walked back toward the couch. When she lounged back down, turning her eyes to him, he gave her a genuine smile and returned to his seat in the chair.

"Good girl."

CHAPTER 7
SHAR

The surfer rubbed his beard while he watched her. His eyes softened slightly from the slate rocks they had become when he got aggravated with her and threatened to walk away. They now held an intensity that was turning her insides to jelly. That look promised a night to remember if she simply complied with his desires. Submission had never been one of her strong points. Though, she'd never before met anyone who demanded it of her in such a way that had her pussy dripping. His eyebrows rose, and she slid her fingers into her bikini bottoms, finding her clit.

Before he had arrived, she was worried she'd have to teach him how to please her, but he wasn't as innocent as he looked. In fact, he was much older than she had originally assessed. Though he had taken her by surprise when he first sat in that chair and commanded her to masturbate, she was glad to find out she was wrong about him.

Without breaking eye contact with him, she took one of her fingers into her mouth, wetting it slightly and then rubbing that moisture into her nipples before she pulled and twisted them. His eyes seemed to grow darker with arousal, and her legs bent up of their own volition as more heat pooled between them. There was something immensely sensual about putting on a show for him.

"I'm waiting." His voice was deep and gravely, and she had to squeeze her legs together to relieve some of the tightness that traveled through her vagina. "Don't close up on me now. Show me what you wish my hands were doing. I know you're not innocent, so let's not play coy."

Shar locked eyes with him and slid her left hand back into her bikini bottoms, her right hand continuing to squeeze her nipples, first one and then the other. When her fingertips grazed across her clit this time, a soft moan escaped her lips. She had already been hot for him when he arrived, and after his dominance at the door, the cloth barely covering her engorged sex was soaked. She wouldn't last much longer with how intently he watched her, but she had no desire to stop. The heat of his eyes on her movements was such a heady turn on. She rubbed her clit in soft circles, increasing the pressure as the desire to close her legs grew.

"Mmmmm that's it. I can see you're finally settling in. Finger yourself."

She tensed. She was equally tired of him telling her what to do if he wasn't going to join her and turned on by his dominance. Her pussy pulsed with each of his commands, leaving her confused about how to respond. She chose the side of pleasure and slid her other hand down from her breasts until she could plunge two fingers into her dripping slit. She pulled her left hand up to her mouth and sucked the taste of her own juices from her fingers, keeping her eyes on him. She moaned again, her arousal growing with each flick of her wrist. For a second, she was so overcome with the sensation that she closed her eyes and threw her head back onto the pillow.

He was standing in front of her with this cock out when she opened her eyes.

"Is this what you want, Pretty?" She went to pull her

hands from her bottoms, and he shook his head. "I didn't tell you to stop. I asked a question."

Her body would not have listened to her mind at this point had she tried to control it. She was too far gone and too horny to not get that cock slammed inside of her. It was beautifully formed with both girth and length, making her mouth water. "Yes."

He smiled and knelt in front of her face. She smiled as her hands went back to work on her pussy, and she opened her mouth to welcome him in. Expecting him to slam his cock to the back of her throat immediately, she was surprised when he placed just the tip between her lips, giving her the chance to run her tongue around it, acclimating to his size. She tightly wrapped her lips around the head, and a small groan left his lips. He slid more of his cock into her mouth, and she opened wider.

"That's it pretty. Open that mouth for my cock!"

Using the hand not guiding his shaft into her mouth, he rubbed her tits, grabbing first one then the other. They weren't overly large, and she often wore pushup bras to make them look proportionate to her hips, but they fit his hands nicely. If her mouth hadn't been full, she might have told him how soft his hands were and how good they felt caressing her pebbled nipples. The most she could do was moan around his cock. His words already had her wetter than she remembered being any time recently, and his touch was just adding to her arousal.

"Are you ready to take it all?" He asked.

She was more than ready and nodded, her hands still working her pussy into a frenzy. Though she wished his cock was filling her pussy, she would gladly take him down her throat.

"Mmmm good girl. Open that mouth and relax your throat."

She didn't need his instructions, but his voice was so

fucking sexy, she nearly came from his words alone. He pulled back until just the tip was in her mouth again and then pushed his hips fully forward. She relaxed and took him to the hilt. He cupped her cheek, and she looked up into his eyes. They were half closed, but he moaned when their eyes locked.

"Yes, that's it's pretty. You're so good at that."

She lowered her eyelids and moaned at his praise. He then wrapped her hair around his hand and began rocking his hips, fucking her mouth, sometimes with shallow strokes and other times until her eyes watered at the fullness in her throat. Her clit was so sensitive, but she continued rubbing over it, knowing she'd be coming soon. Her moans escaped with each thrust of his hips.

"You're going to come, aren't you?" he asked, barely finishing the question before shudders begin to wrack her body.

Coming undone, eyes rolling up into her eyelids, every muscle in her body tightened. She failed to notice when he took his cock out of her mouth, allowing her breath and moans to flow freely. It was a few moments before she came down from the high and opened her eyes to find him staring at her with a shit-eating grin, the fucker. What the hell did she need him for if she had to make herself come. Of course, if she were honest with herself, it wasn't her fingers that did her in. It was him, and she wanted more.

He gave her exactly what she needed, fucking her long into the night. His stamina was unbelievable, better than most of the men half his age that she'd been with. When he finally left her suite, she could hardly move. Her body was sated in the most delightful way. Her muscles were spent, as if she had worked out for hours, and her legs were so wobbly, she barely made it to the bathroom and back. Tomorrow's...no, this morning's shoot would be rough, but she had no regrets. Ok, maybe she had one regret. She should have gotten his contact info. She'd definitely like to see him again.

CHAPTER 8

MACK

Mack's alarm went off way too early, and he groaned at the blaring noise. He hadn't crawled into his bed until the wee hours of the morning. The investors would not be getting his best this morning. He grabbed his phone to silence the alarm and threw it to the other side of the king size bed.

"Fuck me!" he exclaimed to the walls of his suite.

What had he been thinking staying out all night like he was still in his twenties? Ok, he hadn't really been thinking with the logical head. He'd been too busy obsessing over how fucking sexy her orgasms were and how well she took everything he gave to her. Most women tapped out way before he did, but she gave him a run for his money. It was a matter of pride that he wanted to break her, to leave her completely undone. When he'd finally succeeded, he barely made the trip back to his own suite to fall headfirst into the bed.

With an audible groan, he threw back the covers and rolled out of the bed. The sting of the air conditioning caused goosebumps to raise on his arms before he made it to the bathroom to turn on the hot shower. It was enough to wake him fully, allowing his thoughts to focus on the plan for the day. Of course, as soon as he stepped into the hot and steamy shower, all those thoughts turned to last night.

He did not have time to focus on her thick and creamy thighs or the hot wetness of her mouth and pussy. He could not be distracted by thoughts of how well she followed his directions and gave as well as she took. His self-admonishment did not stop his dick from coming to life, though, vying for more attention than a swift once-over with the soapy rag. His fucking dick should be spent, satisfied for at least the rest of the day, if not the week or longer after last night, but no. He pounded on the shower wall in frustration. If he wasn't in a rush, he'd call up to her room and have her come down to take care of it, but there was no time. Taking himself in hand, he punished his incorrigible cock until his release. The growl of dissatisfaction that left his body told him that it would be a while before he got that woman out of his system.

When Mack walked into his morning meeting, the tech investors were already seated at the table. Normally, he liked to arrive super early to get his thoughts together and review the presentation in the room to make sure everything was working properly before anyone else entered. Though he had plastered on a smile and greeted each investor warmly, Mack was feeling anything but warm. Nothing worked out how he had planned it this morning, and he was left to hope that his presentation not only worked but went off without a hitch.

Thankfully, he had the forethought to have his administrative assistant order breakfast, which was delivered just as he began to set up the presentation. This distraction allowed him to make sure everything was working without having all eyes staring at him with impatience. At least, he would have been staring at himself with impatience if he were one of the investors. Instead, they all took the opportunity to indulge in the spread his company provided, relieving some of his tension with their grateful response. He would have to remember to send Janet a bonus for working her magic this morning.

Once everyone was settled, Mack walked them through the previous quarter's numbers. They weren't as good as the projections, and he saw disappointment scattered across the investor's faces.

"What happened to throw the company so far off track?" Stuart Richardson, CEO of Valcon Tech Inc., asked.

"That is a great question, Stuart, and one we have been steadily asking ourselves. We believe that our marketing plan for the Version One phones did not quite meet the mark. Not that it is an excuse, but for the past decade, we have been focused on our services to the tech industry, marketing to other telecommunications companies rather than end users. We believe that we did not make enough of a shift toward the everyday consumer for the devices to take off in the commercial market."

"How do you propose to remedy the situation?" Stuart chimed in again, amidst head nods and agreement from others.

"Thank you for asking. Let me show you our proposed marketing plan for Version Two, which is a significant upgrade from the Version One."

He spent the next hour walking through the marketing plan Kevin devised, and the two of them revised, before Mack had left for California. By the end of the presentation, the investors were smiling and nodding. They could see the vision and were happy to hear that plans were already in place to hire the primary spokesperson.

"My partner assures me that we should have the model on

contract within the week. He is working out the specifics with her agent now, and then it will be sent for her signature."

By the time the investors filed out of the board room, Mack was exhausted. This group had been funding Velocity since its startup days, and their expectations were built on the positive returns the company had earned every year since. This shift in focus and consumer had been difficult for all of them to wrap their heads around. He was hopeful that the afternoon meeting would be an easier sell with their telecommunications investors. They understood the difficulties of marketing a product as opposed to a service, and he suspected they would have suggestions to improve the plan.

Grabbing a crusty bagel on his way out the door, Mack's thoughts turned to the beautiful woman he left asleep this morning. Would she be willing to meet him for dinner? They hadn't exchanged names or contact information. In truth, he hadn't considered the possibility of wanting to see her again. Her napkin invitation said last night was meant to be a one-and-done situation, but he hadn't been able to stop thinking about her. Even during the most contentious parts of his presentation, her soft moans played on loop in his mind. Maybe seeing her again with their clothes on would help get her out of his head.

CHAPTER 9

SHAR

Shar leaned back against the seat as the driver eased them out of the hotel's parking lot. Her mind was going a hundred miles per hour, but her body was still exhausted. Not that she was complaining. She loved the feeling of having been worked over, and he definitely worked her over. The problem was not knowing exactly what type of physical toll this shoot would take. Most of the time her shoots were easy with some minor walking, maybe a little kneeling. Other times, like last week, she had to do some more strenuous physical activity like hiking or jumping on a trampoline.

Pulling out her phone, she brought up Jerry's text thread and asked if he had any of the specifics about today's shoot. Occasionally, the client would send Jerry the specifics, and he would happen to forget to forward her that information. She had never asked for it before, but today was a different day.

> Jerry: No, nothing. Why? Are you alright?

> Yes, just tired. I'll tell you all about it when I see you tomorrow.

> Jerry: You won't be seeing me tomorrow, love. You're traveling.

> ???

The phone rang in her hand, and she answered the call immediately. It had to be something big, else Jerry would've told her via text with more details to come later.

"Why am I traveling tomorrow?"

"Are you sitting down?"

"Jerry, I'm too tired for fucking games today."

"Ooh, bitchy bitchy. You must've gotten your back blown out last night."

"And long into the morning. Now tell me, else I'm going home to sleep for a week."

"Oh yeah, you'll definitely have to give me all the details when I see you, but it won't be tomorrow."

"Jerry!"

"Okay, okay, damn! You are now the proud owner of a year-long contract with multiple marketing campaigns for Velocity Communications."

"What does that mean?"

"That means, your ass is getting paid, girl. You'll be given an advance and held on retainer. You won't have to work for anyone else, though you could, just not in telecommunications. You'll be the primary spokesperson for their Version 2 cell phone release, which means photos and videos, social media posts, and live events. Because you'll be on retainer, they could call on you at any time."

Shar's heart raced, and her stomach fluttered, but she tried to maintain some semblance of calm when all she wanted to do was jump up and down. This was huge, the biggest contract she'd ever gotten. Being the spokesperson for a major product had been one of her dreams for years.

"Jerry, what does that have to do with tomorrow? Are you saying I start working for them tomorrow?"

"You're not as excited as I thought you'd be."

"No, I am, but I'm tired. I'm also confused and worried now about tomorrow. I'll be doing cartwheels later." I gave a small chuckle, and Jerry laughed because I've never done a cartwheel in my life.

"Tomorrow, you fly to the East Coast, and you go in to sign the contract Thursday morning. I'm sending you the electronic copy, but they want a wet signature. While there, you will also have some headshots done and a few test runs with the marketing director, Kevin Dulaney. He will have a car at the airport to pick you up and another waiting at the hotel Thursday morning. I already know how you like to travel, so I've chosen your hotel personally, and I've had them include a couple of extra days. You'll return home Saturday, and I'll meet you for dinner."

Just as Jerry finished giving her the details, the car stopped outside the studio where she'd be working today. "That all sounds good. Send me the specifics because I already checked out of my hotel. Oh, and Jerry..."

She paused for a second after hearing her phone chime that an email had come through. She should have known that he would have not waited until they hung up to send her everything.

"Huh?" He finally asked.

"You're the best!"

She ended the call before he could respond with some sarcastic retort like "I know" or "Of course I am."

"Are you ready to go in, Ms. Maxwell?" the driver asked from the front seat.

Shar took a deep breath to gather her thoughts before responding. She would push through this shoot and then prepare herself for the next phase of her career. A small smile played across her lips as she thought of all Jerry had described, and when her door opened, she let the smile grow wider. Though her muscles were still sore, there was a lightness in her step. Tomorrow would start the year that would change her life.

Since her flight wasn't until the morning, Shar checked into a new hotel after her photoshoot. She looked out the window and quickly closed the curtains. She hated looking out onto the roof of another building or some nondescript skyline. That's why she always had Jerry book her hotels overlooking water. At least then, she'd have something worthwhile to look at. In fact, she'd rather have a 45-minute drive to work than have a miserable view at her hotel.

This view, which overlooked air conditioning units and the open fields of the airport, was depressing. It reminded her of the sad places she'd lived growing up in Beautonville. There was nothing in that dustbowl of a place. Her mother had often been between jobs, barely keeping them fed, so they lived in a slew of rooming houses and motel rooms. That's why she almost always had a suite as well. Spending more than one night in a single room triggered such negative feelings that she'd had to call her therapist more than once. Early in her career, she'd sometimes canceled shoots if she couldn't get her mind right because of the visceral response of staying in the wrong hotel.

The new gig would change everything. She'd be returning to the same place multiple times, staying at the same hotels, and making enough money to relax some days without having to hustle these small one-day gigs just to ensure her home was safe. This was her big break.

For the first time since Jerry's call, Shar thought of the

surfer. They hadn't done much talking at all, but she found herself wondering whether she'd have seen him again had she checked back into that same hotel tonight. Would they have maybe met for dinner, exchanged names, or simply enjoyed each other for another night. He had looked genuinely remorseful when he got up to go back to his room early this morning, so she doubted he was as married to the one-night-stand life as she was. How would seeing him again have felt? "Oh well," she said aloud to the empty room. There was no use in dwelling on the coulda, shoulda or woulda now that it would definitely be a year or more before she'd be back this way.

Her brain didn't listen to that logic, though, and when she woke in the morning to shower for her flight, he was still on her mind. Her body responded to the memories of his demands, creating a near-painful ache between her thighs. The warm water and suds flowing over her body did nothing to staunch the heat gathering in her core. She thought of his command to touch herself, and she let her hand slide down between her legs. Before long, she was leaned against the shower wall shuddering as she exploded around her fingers, wishing it was his cock and hoping he would now be out of her system.

Hopping out of the shower, she toweled off and threw on some travel clothes. She always traveled as comfortably as possible. Today's outfit was black leggings, a band t-shirt, a hoodie, and some sneakers. She didn't even bother doing her makeup, just threw her hair in a bun and called for a ride to the airport. People who got all dolled up to sit in a stuffy airport and then on a cramped plane were an enigma to her. She'd have plenty of time for that once she arrived at her destination and checked into the hotel. Sometimes, they cut the time close, but since all her shoots included someone else doing her hair and makeup, it never took her much time to get ready at the hotel.

CHAPTER 10
MACK

When Mack finally got back to the hotel, he was exhausted and cranky. Normally, he'd have changed into his swim trunks or wetsuit and been on a board within twenty minutes. Today, though, he'd spent every free minute thinking about the woman he'd left asleep early that morning. After a quick shower, he stepped out on the balcony and tried to scan the collection of chaise for her. When he couldn't find her, he sat on the bed trying to decide the best way to contact her. They hadn't discussed the possibility of hooking up again, so while he was secure in himself, he didn't want to just show up at her room.

Before he could talk himself out of it and find something else to do, Mack picked up the phone and dialed Suite 316. There was no answer. "Shit!" He eyed the surfboard that leaned against the wall. He should've just gone out on the water and let the entire day wash away with the waves. That wasn't what he wanted to do though. He wanted some company. Kevin would be ragging on him something awful if he knew. Mack had never been one to crave the company of a woman. That's why he was still single after all these years, even with women throwing themselves at his money. With an irritated sigh, he grabbed his keycard and made his way toward the elevator.

"Good afternoon, Mr. Mackenzie. No time on the water today?"

"Not today, Bruno. In fact, I was hoping you could help me."

"Of course. What do you need?"

"I'm trying to find the woman in Suite 316. I called her room, but no one answered."

Bruno tapped on his tablet a few times before looking back up.

"I'm sorry, sir. That room is vacant."

"What do you mean?" Mack asked, his voice sounding far more desperate than he'd intended.

"It looks like that guest checked out this morning."

Mack stared at him, flabbergasted. When he'd left her around 2am, she had been knocked out. She hadn't mentioned leaving today. Then again, they hadn't done much talking at all. They hadn't even exchanged names.

"Bruno, is there any way..."

Bruno shook his head before Mack could finished the question. "I'm sorry, Mr. Mackenzie, but I cannot give you any information about another guest."

Mack sighed, thanked Bruno, and headed back toward his room. His irritation was a living thing inside of him. Though he'd grown up wanting, he had grown used to getting what he wanted since starting his business. The fact that he wanted this woman whose name he hadn't bothered to ask, and the fact that she was inaccessible didn't set well with him. Just as he was punching the button to call the elevator, someone shouted from behind him.

"Mack, wait up."

Recognizing the voice, Mack turned to see April Murphy, the daughter of one of his investors sauntering toward him. She was as stunning as ever. Her red hair bouncing with each stride was complemented by a pencil skirt and green silk blouse. Her makeup was flawless and her green eyes shone like emeralds. She oozed old money and wore that power like armor.

"Hello, April. What a surprise to see you here," Mack said, trying to read her intentions.

They had history. The first time he came to California to meet with her father, she had been at his office. She'd followed Mack outside after the meeting and offered to put in a good word with her father if he acted as her date for some social event he couldn't even remember anymore. He was much younger and a bit naiver. He'd needed investors so bad back then, he'd have done just about anything. The social event led to a sexual awakening for Mack. She was the one who taught him to be dominant, taught him to take as a way of giving. She also taught him to not tie sex to emotions.

"Why didn't you tell me you were in town? I happened to overhear my father talking about this morning's meeting. You're not avoiding me, are you?"

He watched her carefully. There was a challenge in that last question. He'd had enough of being challenged today, enough of not feeling in control of what was happening. Though he'd never admit it, today's meetings had taken a toll. He felt his frustration from the meetings boil up and mix with his irritation at having that woman slip out of his grasp.

"If I had been avoiding you, I would have gotten on the elevator without stopping."

He raised a brow, and she looked down, shifting the power dynamic to him. He'd be lying if he said her goading and control of her emotions didn't turn him on. Everything she did was methodical, even her submission, and he wished he could exude that much control.

"Suite 518," he said.

A smile played at the corner of her mouth before she masked her expression and looked up at him. He gave a slight nod in response, and she summoned the elevator. When the doors opened, she pressed the fifth-floor button and looked to him for instruction.

"Have you been a good girl since the last time I saw you, April?"

"No, sir. I have not."

Her eyes held no remorse, and he gave her a lecherous grin.

"Tell me, do you want to be punished or rewarded?"

She smiled for the first time since the game started, and his mind played over the previous times she'd come to him rejoicing in her own bad behavior. She'd wanted to role-play punishment as a reward. Since they had no true relationship, nothing binding them together, this was the type of game she liked to play whenever she could catch him out here. He didn't exactly lie when he said he wasn't avoiding her because he never intentionally sought her out. Now that she was here, though, he would take advantage of the situation.

"Everything off, except your panties," he said as she opened the door to the room.

He pushed the door shut and walked past without looking her way. He already knew she would do as he said because this was her element. He pulled the ottoman from the chair in the corner and set it in front of the couch. Looking up at her standing just inside the doorway, naked from the waist up, he started to roll up his sleeves.

"You said that you have not been a good girl and that you wish to be rewarded with punishment. Is that right?"

She lifted her chin. She could never fully submit. It just wasn't in her, no matter how much she tried. The defiance was too strong. The power was too ingrained thanks to her father's position and money. She just liked to pretend. He knew this, and he played along. He knew that he was a safe space for her to play out these fantasies, though sometimes he wanted to break her. He'd seen someone else do it once, and his balls tightened at the memory. It took all his restraint not to rub his cock through his pants when she finally responded.

"Yes, sir."

"Would you like to confess your transgressions? We can determine an appropriate punishment for each one."

"There are many," she said, her voice husky and seductive.

"I have all night. Now, get on your knees and crawl to the confessional."

She slowly lowered herself to the floor and made her way across the room to the sitting area. When she reached the ottoman, she sat back on her heels.

"Forgive me, sir, for I have been very naughty in your absence."

He waited for her to continue. Though her head was bowed, as she continued to play the part, the corner of her mouth was visible enough for him to catch the lift of a smile.

"I invited a couple to my apartment. I seduced the wife and convinced her to let me tie her husband to a chair. Then I did things to her body he could only dream of doing. My hands and tongue were everywhere on her, but all of my attention was on his response. His breathing was ragged, and his cock strained against his jeans until a small dark spot developed where he was leaking. It was erotic knowing he wished he could be in the mix with us but was stuck."

"Did the wife not beg for mercy for her poor, horny husband?"

"She never even looked in his direction until I had wrung multiple orgasms from her body. In the end, her clit was so sensitive, she begged me to stop. It was I who had pity on the man. I offered to ride his cock while she licked my clit until I came."

Mack's eyes narrowed at her boldness, doubting the truth of her story, but he knew how she played the game. "Did you expect him to last that long after watching you pleasuring his wife in ways he couldn't, or rather probably hadn't?"

"That was the caveat I put in place. I told him there was one rule. If he came, not only would I punish him harshly, but I would ensure his wife left so sore, she wouldn't let him touch her for weeks. Of course, he agreed."

He leaned toward her from where he was sitting, his cock begging for release. "And what punishment do you think you deserve for this behavior?"

"I deserve to be spanked until my ass is red from your hand and my pussy drips from the sting."

So be it, he thought, grabbing her shoulders and pressing her down across the ottoman. She had on bikini cut bottoms that covered a good deal of her ass. Rather than remove them, he pulled them inward until the material was scrunched between her cheeks. If she moved too much, they would rub uncomfortably.

"Count," he said, and brought his hand down on the left side.

His dick pulsed with each number she said, but he didn't stop. Not until he had fulfilled her request of making her pussy drip. She made it to 20 in her count. He ran his hand down along her slit, gathering her juices before rubbing her ass to soothe the skin.

"Do you have more to confess?"

"Yes." She was panting.

"What toys did you bring in that bag of yours? Crawl over there and bring them back to me one at a time."

When she didn't move right away, he thought she would deny his request, but then she turned away from him. She pulled the first item from her bag and started to make her way back to him.

"Carry it in your mouth."

"Sir?"

"Put each of your toys in your mouth, so that you can crawl unimpeded."

She sat up on her heels and stared into his eyes before bringing the butt plug to her mouth. He was not concerned about her consternation because he knew she was meticulous in cleaning her toys after each use. She crawled over to him and dropped the plug into his hand. When she turned to head back toward her bag, he stopped her.

"Let's not waste this," he said with a menacing grin. "Be a good girl and lean back over the ottoman like you were moments ago."

He stood and walked toward her bag. What he was hoping she had was sitting right in the open, and he grabbed it. He returned to his place on the couch and caressed her ass. He pulled her panties down around her thighs and spread her ass cheeks. Flipping open the small bottle in his hand, he squirted some of the lube on her puckered hole. Her breath caught when the cool liquid ran across her hot skin. When he worked the lube around her hole and slowly pressed the tight spot, she sighed. Her arousal was evident, as juices ran from her pussy, and he knew she would be ready to come soon.

"Do not come until I'm inside of you," he commanded. When she whimpered, he repeated the expectation. "If you come before your pussy clenches my dick, I will kick you out of my suite wearing only what you have on. Do you understand?"

She took a deep breath and finally agreed.

"Good girl. Now let's get your ass filled like you like it."

He pressed his thumb further into her hole and then pulled it out to gather more lube. Each time, he pushed a little further, working it in small circles until he slipped past the tight bands holding it closed. A moan escaped her lips, and Mack slapped her ass.

"Don't forget what I told you."

He worked his thumb in and out of her asshole until she was panting. She loved anal. He'd learned that very early on in their friendship. When his thumb no longer met resistance each time he pulled it out and reinserted it, he released her cheeks to pick up the butt plug. She whined, and he slapped her ass again. This time, she yelped in surprise, and he smiled.

"Are you ready to have your ass filled, naughty girl?"

"Yes," she managed to squeak out between quick breaths.

"What was that?" He'd heard her, but part of the game was to make her repeat herself when she was teetering on the edge.

"Yes, please fill my ass."

He squirted ample lube on the plug and rubbed it around from pointed tip to the roundest part of the bulb. Once again, spreading her cheeks, he lined up the tip, and slowly pushed it through the puckered entrance. When she held her breath, as the bulb widened her opening, he slid two fingers into her wet pussy to distract her. He worked his fingers in and out, curling the tips while he pushed the bulb into her ass until it popped in place, her sphincter closing around it.

"Mmmmm look at how beautifully your ass swallowed that bulb. I'm so proud of you, I'm going to reward you with my cock."

He pulled her panties back up, making sure to situate the material, so her cheeks were still exposed. The pressure against the plug would add to her pleasure. He helped her up to sit back on her heels and then pulled his cock out of his pants. Her eyes were hooded in arousal, and when she looked up at his erection, pure lust flitted across her face.

"Put your hands on your thighs and keep them there," he said before moving closer. "Now open that naughty mouth of yours."

When she opened her mouth and dropped her tongue, he slid the tip of his cock between her lips. She moaned and swirled her tongue around it. He grabbed a handful of her hair and pulled her mouth onto his dick. She didn't gag, just took him to the hilt.

"Yes, you're so damn good at that. Now, hold that mouth open."

They both moaned as he began fucking her mouth. He poured the days frustrations into each thrust reaching for that sweet release that would leave him spent. When she moaned, though, he remembered that she was holding off waiting for him.

"Fuck," he growled and pulled his dick from her mouth. "Grab a condom."

She nearly ran to her bag, but he noticed her movements were a little slower than usual. He had left her on her knees far too long. Though she wouldn't complain, guilt began to fester in his abdomen. This game was meant to be a give and take, and he forgot that, forgot himself in his frustration. He stood when she walked back toward him, open condom in hand. He allowed her to put it on him, and then, instead of returning her to her knees, he bent her over the arm of the couch, so her ass was in the air. The metal knob of the plug showing between her cheeks.

She'd not spoken since he'd inserted the plug. Normally, that wouldn't have bothered him, but he wanted to make sure she was still good. "Hard or soft?" he asked as he lined the tip of his cock to her entrance. She made a soft mewling sound and wiggled her ass. "Use your words. Do you want it hard or soft?"

She looked back at him and licked her lips. Her eyes gleaming, she said, "Hard."

Between her own slickness and remnants of the lube he'd used earlier, he slid in effortlessly. Then he did give it to her hard. Pulling her arms back by the elbows to give him more leverage, he pounded into her. She came almost immediately, but he gave her no reprieve. When he let her arms go, he grabbed a fistful of her hair and continued the onslaught. Her moans turned to screams of his name, as she came again before he finally felt his balls tighten. Heat coursed through his body, and a scream of his own tore from his throat as he came.

Mack waited until both of them had caught their breath and his heart rate returned to a somewhat normal level before pulling out of her and heading toward the bathroom. After flushing the condom, he took a hot shower, willing his body to fully relax. When he left the bathroom, his eyes widened, and his throat constricted. April was still splayed across the arm of the couch where he'd left her. Where he'd forgotten about her.

"Shit," he said aloud. "Get up and go shower."

She did as he said, and when she returned, he told her to dress. She looked to him with sad eyes, and the pit in his stomach grew. April wasn't needy, and she had never wanted more than they shared, but she did like to pretend they were more afterward. He didn't have it in him tonight.

"Look, I'm sorry. I lost track of the game. Today did not go the way I'd wanted at all, and you walked in at the wrong..." or maybe the right time, he thought to himself. "the wrong time offering a reprieve from the frustrations of the day. I took advantage of that."

"Took advantage?" she asked with a sardonic chuckle. "I came here wanting exactly what you gave, and I was not disappointed until this moment. What the fuck is wrong with you, Sloan Mackenzie? You act like you just cheated on your wife and guilt set in."

She could have thrown ice water on him, and it would not have stung more. What was this guilt he was feeling? Granted, April hadn't been the woman he'd thought about all day or the one he'd wanted when the night started, but he didn't even know that woman. There was no reason for his guilt.

"Go home, April."

She was already dressing. When she gathered up her belongings, the plug conspicuously missing and likely still in her ass, she turned back to him.

"You're a real shit sometimes, Mack."

Then she was out the door.

He leaned his head back against the couch cushion. He sure felt like shit. Looking out at the setting sun, he turned toward the bedroom to find his wetsuit.

CHAPTER 11

SHAR

"**M**on petit chaton, I did not expect to see you here."
Shar looked up at the familiar voice to see Henri standing in the aisle next to her row on the plane. He winked and lifted a bag into the overhead compartment. She was left to stare at his torso, which was perfectly outlined by his tailored button-down shirt tucked into the waistband of trousers tailored in the beautifully European way of leaving little to the imagination. Her mouth watered as she took him in. Then she remembered that she was dressed like a ragamuffin.

He took the seat next to her, grabbed her hand and brought it to his mouth. Oh, he was smooth. "You look even more lovely this morning. Casual with tousled hair like you were well-fucked suits you."

Heat rose in her cheeks, and she looked away before he could see her smile. Yeah, he was smooth and perceptive. She knew she shouldn't just leave him hanging after a statement like that, but she needed to tamp down her libido. She appreciated the boldness of this man. Between the feel of his soft lips on her hand and his accent, she was ready to join the mile high club, all thoughts of the surfer drifting out to sea. When his seatbelt clicked, she chanced a glance in his direction, and he was still looking at her with a raised brow. She couldn't hold back her smile and raised her own brow in response.

Just then a flight attendant came by asking if they'd like a beverage. Though it was 7:30am, they both ordered something with a kick. Why not? She had plenty to celebrate, and maybe he'd be the bow, or maybe she could get him to wear one.

"Business or pleasure?"

"Pardon?"

"Is your trip for business or pleasure?"

"Oh," he says with a sly grin, "I'm hoping for a little of both. You?"

"I'm traveling for business, but I never mind adding a little pleasure into these trips."

He smiled, and his beautiful eyes sparkled. The plane taxied down the runway, and she laid her head back against the seat. Though Shar always chose a window seat, so she could look out at the passing landscape, she hated the feel of taking off and landing. She looked over at her unexpected companion, and his hands were tightly folded in his lap, a slight grimace on his face. Apparently, she wasn't the only one affected by the directional change. While she wasn't scared, her stomach always twinged a bit as soon as the plane lifted off. His response appeared far stronger. She put her hand on his, and he enveloped it between them.

Once the plane leveled off, he squeezed her hand and then let it go. Shar reached down into her bag and pulled out an e-reader for the ride. She wasn't sleepy, but she needed something more than alcohol to pass the next six hours. Now, if only she could make a quick decision of which book to choose. Was she in the mood for a dark academia with ghoul fucking, a medical drama where things get heated, or a fun monster romance with gargoyles and a witch who can't do magic? All her moods were a little spicy, she mused while pressing the power button.

"Merci," Henri whispered near her ear.

She smiled up at him. "No worries. I struggle with takeoffs too."

"Really? You looked completely relaxed."

"I do that to control my breathing. Hyperventilating in a metal tube is not a good look," she said with a chuckle. "I did that my very first time on a plane, and I almost passed out. If my agent didn't book me jobs all over this country, I'd probably have never flown again after that. It was embarrassing as hell."

"Merde. I can only imagine."

"Yeah, so you're doing well," she gave him another small smile before turning my attention back to the device in my hand.

The flight attendant brought them breakfast and another drink. Henri pulled out his phone, and Shar leaned back to settle in for a couple hours of losing herself in the paranormal world. Thank goodness those devices tracked the last page read because she'd never have remembered. Trying to make sense of where she was in the story, she flipped back a couple pages to the library scene, and the pulsing between her thighs reminded her of exactly what had happened last. Yep, just what she needed.

Shar had no idea how much time had passed when she felt Henri's breath on her shoulder and neck. Was he falling asleep? She was in the middle of a very dark and steamy scene and was a bit miffed at being interrupted. When she turned her head to look at him, though, his eyes were wide open, staring at the device in her hand. He was reading over her shoulder. Shit! He lifted his eyes to hers, and she could read the lust in them. His behavior, the audacity to invade her space and invade her privacy, should've been a turn off, but she was already wet from what was transpiring on the page.

"Your breathing was getting heavy, and I was worried that something was wrong," he said against her neck.

She closed her eyes at the sensation. "How long have you been reading along with me?" Was it only this scene or the previous one as well? She wasn't going to ask for specific details. His lips this close to her skin already had her heartbeat skipping.

"Just a couple of pages. Enough to recognize why your breathing had changed. You like knife play?"

She shook her head vigorously. "No, only on paper. I have some very hard limits. I prefer to be worshipped."

She didn't have to see his face to feel the smile that spread across his lips. He ran his nose up along the length of her neck and to her ear.

"Let me get on my knees for you, mon petit chaton," he whispered, his lips on her earlobe. "I will make you purr for me."

"I have a meeting in the morning, but I could be convinced to meet you for dinner."

"I, too, have a meeting in the morning. Dessert sounds wonderful."

Without another word, Henri sat back in his seat and closed his eyes. Shar squeezed her thighs together and turned her attention back to the story. This day was turning out better than expected.

She and Henri had agreed to meet at a restaurant close to his hotel before they left the plane. Thankfully, Velocity had assigned her a driver for the entire time she'd be in the area, so she wouldn't have to take a cab. Since her hotel was on an island off the coast and not in the city, cab rides could get costly. Not that she couldn't afford it, especially if everything in the contract Jerry sent her was true. She hadn't signed that contract yet, though, so she would not count on that money. One of the few lessons her mother had taught her that she still applied to her life was to never count money you didn't yet hold.

Speaking of money, the fountain outside of her hotel probably cost more than her entire apartment building when it was first built. The thing was massive with a statue of Poseidon and his trident in the middle, water splashing all around like he had just sprung forth from the ocean. Once again, she envisioned tousled dark blonde hair, similar in color to her own, popping out of the ocean after he had wiped out on his surfboard. There had just been something about him that called to her. Hopefully, an evening with Henri would put the sexy stranger out of her mind. She didn't feel the same pull toward Henri, so he was safe.

Thanks to the time change, it was already late afternoon by the time she got out of the shower and dressed for dinner. She chose a long-line sundress that hugged her curves and accentuated her relatively small breasts. She couldn't wear a bra with this dress, so she was grateful for how it molded to her body. Rather than a pair of heels, she opted for some cute flat sandals that allowed her to be comfortable and yet still look polished. She pulled her long hair back into a tight bun and applied some mascara and tinted lip balm before grabbing her bag and heading back downstairs to the lobby.

She'd asked her driver to pick her up for dinner at 6:30, and he was right on time. She doubted he'd even left the island. The ride to the restaurant took forty minutes, and she used the time to listen to an audiobook. This time, she opted for a space opera with intrigue and outrageous technology.

The book she had chosen on the plane had plenty of spice, so this book would balance it out nicely.

"Fred, I'm meeting a friend for dinner and not sure what time I'll be ready to return to the hotel or if I'll even be leaving from this location. What is the latest you work for me to call you?"

"I am on call for whenever you need me, Ms. Maxwell."

Shar smiled at him through the rearview mirror. "I understand that, but I also would feel terrible waking you at 2am to come drive me somewhere."

"No, please, do not feel bad. That is my job, and it is much safer that you call me than a cab or some other ride-share in the middle of the night. Please call me."

With a nod, Shar agreed. When they pulled up to the restaurant, Henri was standing outside waiting for her. He broke into a huge smile when Fred helped her down from the vehicle. She smiled back.

"I was afraid you would not come. How far away is your hotel?"

"Your offer was so generous, how could I not? The ride wasn't too long."

She did not want to tell him where she was staying. The island hideaway would stay just that. Jerry knew she didn't ever want to be that close to the job site, and she preferred an ocean view. Not everyone had that opportunity with their gigs, so she kept her plans to herself.

"Is your hotel far from here?" she asked, as much making conversation as trying to judge where they'd go for this dessert he'd promised.

"Not at all. I was able to walk. It is a beautiful evening, yes?"

She nodded in agreement and took his offered arm to enter the restaurant. He must have called ahead because they were seated right away. Their booth was semi-secluded in a dim corner with soft music playing through the speaker overhead.

It was quiet enough they could hear each other but loud enough others couldn't overhear their conversation. The thought that maybe he'd been here before passed through her mind, but the server arrived to take their drink order before she could ask.

The booth was circular, and even though they had each gotten in at different ends, Henri moved himself around until he was seated close enough to put his hand on her knee. He lowered his head to her ear.

"I have been thinking of you all afternoon. You looked belle this morning, but you are simply stunning tonight, and you smell..." He sniffed her neck right behind her ear before finishing with, "delicious."

The man did know the art of seduction. Each word and each move was calculated. While she didn't feel genuine passion from him, she had no doubt that he also understood how to please a woman. Nothing about him gave off a selfish vibe. Still, something was gnawing at her.

The server brought their food, and they set to savoring the delicious meal. Shar was impressed with Henri's choice of restaurant and his suggestion for entrees to try.

"Do you come here often?" she asked, wondering if he was maybe from the area.

"No," he said with a sly laugh. "I asked for a recommendation at the hotel, and they suggested this restaurant. Then others shared their favorite meals here. It was a good choice, yes?"

"Yes, a very good choice. I was just thinking since you said you were here for a meeting and knew this great place that maybe you were here regularly."

He shook his head and took another bite of his chicken cacciatore. Then he moved in conspiratorially before she could prepare herself and said, "I am here to sign a contract with Velocity Communications. No one is supposed to know yet, but I trust you not to tell my secrets."

Shar had just taken a bite of her shrimp carbonara and proceeded to choke on it, her gasp having caused a piece to lodge in her windpipe. Henri did not seem to notice at first, continuing to talk about how everything surrounding the contract and the plans were very hush hush. All he knew from his agent was that he would be working with someone who was said to be a star in the making. As he talked, Shar did everything to catch her breath. She took a sip of her wine because it was closest to her hand. Then she tried gulping from her water glass. Finally, she held up a finger at him and nearly ran to the bathroom.

After a short coughing fit, she sneezed twice, and she could breathe again. She wasn't sure she wanted to breathe. Fuck, he was going to be her co-star in these marketing ads. No. She should've known. With her hands on each side of the sink, she looked at herself in the mirror. Dammit, Shar, why couldn't you have asked him on the plane? Why couldn't you have told him to hold off dinner until tomorrow, after you both went to your respective meetings? Why did you always have to get your groove on before a job instead of after? She didn't stop silently berating herself until someone walked into the restroom. She took a deep breath, stood up straight, and returned to the table.

"Is everything alright, mon petit chaton?" he asked, picking up his fork.

She hesitated a moment before answering. "Yes and no, Henri."

With the forkful of food almost to his mouth, he looked at her serious expression and put it back on the plate. "What is wrong? Are we not having a good dinner?"

"It has been a wonderful dinner, and I hope what I'm about to say does not ruin our ability to work together."

He sat up straighter, a confused look on his face. "Work together. Work was not what we were planning, I didn't think."

"No, it wasn't, but it is now," she said plainly. "I, too, am signing a contract with Velocity tomorrow."

He visibly relaxed. "Oh, that is wonderful, chere. We'll be able to see each other often."

"Too often," she said under her breath. To him, she said, "Yes, we will, and seeing each other for work is all we'll be able to do."

He tilted his head to the side, and she watched as he seemed to turn over her words. It took several moments, but she read when disappointment dawned in him. He opened his mouth and then closed it again. He clearly wanted to say something, but there wasn't anything he could say that would change her mind.

"This has nothing to do with you," she offered, trying to smooth things over. She didn't forget that he never noticed her choking, but that was unimportant right now. "I do not shit where I eat." His brows once again furrowed in confusion. He looked down at the plate in front of her and then back to her face. "I don't fuck around at work." When he still didn't seem to fully understand her metaphors, she clarified, "I do not have sex with coworkers."

"Oh," was all he said after a full minute of uncomfortable silence. Then he picked up his fork and placed the forgotten bite in his mouth. "Finish your dinner. This delicious meal is not to be wasted."

"I hope this awkward situation will not ruin our ability to work together over the length of this contract." Under the table, she wrung her hands together. This was her first long contract, and she hated the idea that it would be tainted by unrequited desire. Hopefully, he really did understand the reason for her boundary.

"Oh mon petit chaton, I am a professional. Besides, like all contracts, this one will eventually end. Maybe we can revisit tonight when it does."

His earlier disappointment transformed into one of hope,

and then he settled into a neutral cordiality. She watched his fluctuating emotions with fascination. She could take lessons in expression from him. When he continued his meal with a smile on his face, she finally picked up her fork and joined him. Between bites, she sent a text to her driver to pick her up. She could use a walk on the beach.

CHAPTER 12

MACK

Mack decided to cut his trip short. He had done all he came to do and made an ass out of himself. It was time to go home. Once he got off the phone with Kevin and verified there was little chance he'd make it to the office before their two stars signed the contracts and were gone for the evening, he called Janet to change his flight to tomorrow morning.

"You're coming back early? That's unusual."

"Thank you for reminding me, Janet. I like to try and surprise you occasionally."

She snorted. He knew he never really surprised the woman. She had worked for them for too long, and she knew every move they made. Hell, he wouldn't be surprised if she knew that he had been with two different women that weekend and regretted one of them.

"I didn't realize it before, but both people Kevin is meeting with flew in from that same airport the other day. How ironic that you all should have been in the same place. They could have just signed the contracts with you and saved us some travel funds."

"That is interesting. I'm not worried about the travel, though. We have plenty in the budget for that."

"Oh, I know. Else you couldn't be changing your plans to suit your mood. Anyway, your flight now leaves at 6:45am."

"Thanks, Janet," he said and ended the call.

He quickly dialed his driver and set up an early pick-up time, so he wouldn't miss his flight and began to pack. He was ready to get away from the memories he'd made here this trip. He didn't need the distraction of regret and resentment. He also didn't want to think too much about the response of his investors. Their questions made him uncomfortable, especially that first group. For the first time since they had begun working together, he got the feeling they didn't trust him to make money anymore, like he was making bad decisions for the business. He knew they were moving in the right direction by differentiating their offerings and establishing themselves as more than just service providers, but he had failed to make them see it. Maybe he should have sent Kevin. If he had, he wouldn't have met the woman of his dreams or made the mistake he made with April.

With that negative thought in mind, he called for room service rather than making his way downstairs, and he flipped on the TV. Of course, one of the first commercials he saw was for his competitor. It was good. Much better than anything they had put out in the last year for their Version 1. They really did fail to market that device properly. This year had to be better. He trusted Kevin wholeheartedly. He also saw and admitted that he hadn't done enough research into what the market was expecting. They had thought to succeed on their past successes, to let their name stand on its own. The only problem was that not enough people knew their name or knew that they were the name behind their favorite brands. That had to change. For that reason, he wanted someone else to be the face of the product, the face people put with the device. He needed to remain the primary face of the company, including their services. Hopefully, Kevin's choices were up for the task, and there wouldn't bet be any setbacks in them giving their all for the company.

Once he was packed and had something in his stomach, Mack jumped in the shower and flopped on the bed. Game shows played in the background. If he couldn't sleep, he'd watch some trivia. If he could sleep, trivia would watch him.

His plane had been delayed an hour. As soon as he landed in Wrighton Springs, Mack headed straight to the office. The building would be closing soon, but he had a key. He wanted to check in with Kevin and Janet, if they were still there. Thankfully, they were.

"How'd things go today? Are the stars onboard?"

"Well, hello to you too, Mr. Mackenzie," Janet said with a disapproving look.

She acted like his mother sometimes. If his mother were still alive, she'd probably be scolding him regularly too, so he'd let Janet take her place in that role. As it was, he couldn't handle two older women disappointed in him. One was quite sufficient, and since he couldn't seem to keep a woman his age or younger around, it just felt that much worse.

"Good evening, Janet," he said with a sigh.

She shook her head at him, but before she could say anything, Kevin came in close and clapped him on the shoulder. "Everything here went great. They are both excited to be working with us. They shared that they had worked well together before, so that shouldn't be a problem, and they are ready to clear their calendars at the drop of a hat when we're ready to get started."

"Wonderful," Mack said quietly. "And they're doing the

test shots when? I'd like to have a meeting with them and the board while they're here."

Kevin eyed him. "Did everything go okay in California? You seem less enthusiastic than I had hoped at the news."

Mack sighed again. "I know you're getting ready to go home, but do you have a few minutes?"

"Is this going to ruin my whole night? Tabitha and I have tickets to a show, and she will have my balls if I'm in a bad mood throughout the whole thing."

Laughing, Mack responded, "No, I don't think it will ruin your night, but I think that getting it off my chest and listening to you tell me I'm overthinking it all will help me sleep better tonight."

Kevin didn't seem convinced, but he agreed. As they made their way toward Mack's office, Mack yelled over his shoulder, "Go home, Janet. We can catch up tomorrow." Mack felt her eyes on his back until he was through the door and out of eyeshot.

Kevin sat on one of the chairs in the center of the room. Instead of going to his desk, Mack took the other chair and turned it toward his friend.

"All right," Kevin said, "lay it on me. What the hell happened?"

"Every fucking thing!"

Mack proceeded to tell him about the meetings with the investors and how differently they went, as well as his interpretation of their questions and responses. As he expected, Kevin told him that he was overthinking it and worrying about nothing. That helped him feel a little better. Then he told Kevin about the situation with the investor's daughter. Kevin knew all about their on-again, off-again flings, but he seemed more interested than usual this time.

"Why are you telling me about this now? Not that I don't like to hear about your fun times, now that I'm over the hill and shackled to the love of my life, but this is usually what happens between you two, right?"

"Well, yes, except..." He trailed off.

"Except what?" Kevin asked, his voice lilting in exasperation. "It's not like you to be so dramatic."

"Except, I purposely didn't tell her I was there. I didn't tell her I was coming. And, Kev, there was someone else."

"Someone else?" His brows rose dangerously close to his hairline, or at least where his hairline had been before it started retreating from his face.

"Yes. When I got there the first night, I did what I normally do, jumped out of my clothes and got on my board. When I left the ocean, there was this stunning woman with tanned skin and a yellow bathing suit sitting out in the setting sun."

Kevin quietly waited for Mack to continue. Mack swallowed and then proceeded to explain how she was there again the next day, and she invited him to her room. He didn't give Kevin all the details about what happened that night, but he made sure that his partner understood how their encounter had affected him. The fact that he wanted her again was a big deal. Normally, he didn't return to random encounters.

Kevin remained silent, and he wondered what the other man was thinking. There was no reason he shouldn't have something to say.

"Why aren't you saying anything?"

"I was waiting for you to finish. Are you telling me that's it?"

"What do you mean? I told you that I met her and then she just left. She didn't even tell me she was leaving that next day. I wanted to see her again. Hell, I had spent the entire day thinking about her. All through that hellscape of meetings with the investors, all I kept thinking about was seeing her again. I actually wanted to take her to dinner."

"Wait, hold up!" Kevin said, putting a hand in the air.

"You wanted to what? Take her to dinner? Not just to bed again? Now that is something. What was it about this woman that had you so enthralled?"

That was a great question and one he hadn't spent the time exploring. "That right there is the important question, isn't it? I don't know."

"Well, go home, maybe go for a walk on the beach, and think it over. I bet if you can come up with a reason, you'll be able to let it go."

"Maybe. Thanks, man. We'll talk through more of the plans tomorrow, and we'll need to set up a timeline for bringing the stars back in for a true start to the campaigns."

"Their test shots are scheduled for Friday, but I doubt I can get the board together before Monday. I'll reach out and reschedule with them. We'll just lengthen their hotel stays and have Janet reschedule their flights."

With that, Kevin walked out the door with a wave over his head. Neither of them bothered to say goodbye. Their friendship and partnership didn't need formalities. Mack stood and considered turning on his computer. Then he shook his head and spun on his heel. He would take Kevin's advice and go for a walk on the beach. He needed to get his mind cleared.

CHAPTER 13
MACK

Mack slipped off his flip-flops as he walked down the sand path to the beach. Though he lived on the island, and his house backed up to the bay, he didn't want to just sit outside and watch the water. He wanted to put his feet in the sand and let the waves wash over his toes. He needed the sound of the surf to settle his mind. It was too late to bring out his board and get in the water. He might be a bit of a daredevil, but he didn't have a death wish. An empty beach at night where no one could hear your cries for help was not a safe place to be surfing.

He liked the area behind the large hotel set off from the rest. It was nestled and quiet, even midday. Most people preferred to stay at hotels closer to the strip where all the bars and activities for the kids were located, but he didn't gain any pleasure from those things. In fact, they bored him most of the time, which is why he had built his house even further down the island away from all of that. He looked up at the ten-story building that spread out on both sides of the elevator shaft like an open book. This hotel only offered suites, so each of the balconies led into a kitchenette and then the bedrooms were closer to the street side. He'd made his way down here years ago when he first moved to the island, and one of the housekeepers let him inside to see the amenities. Okay, maybe it wasn't the amenities she wanted to show him, but he got the full view of everything, including her and one of her coworkers. He was much younger then. At 39, he felt so much older.

He was almost directly behind the hotel when he noticed a shadow walking down the walkway toward the beach. He couldn't see anything more than the outline of a woman with long hair blowing in the breeze. She nearly barreled into him when she exited the dunes because she hadn't noticed him walking.

"Oh, I'm so sorry. I didn't see you."

His hands had encircled her arms to hold them both steady, so they didn't tumble into the sand together. "No harm done," he said and released her. She turned herself fully in his direction and looked up at him, her face finally showing in the moonlight. It was her.

"You," he said, his voice a whisper, like she might disappear if he spoke too loudly.

Her head tilted to the side. "Do I know you?" she asked, unnerved by his change in tone.

"We've met." He reached out a hand toward her, but she stepped back at his sudden movement in the shadows. She didn't scream or run, though, so hopefully, that was a good sign. "I promise, if we turn, I won't be in the shadows, and you'll be able to see my face." He started to walk around her, keeping the same distance in the entire arc of his path. She followed him with her eyes first, and then her body slowly joined. Once he knew he was in position, he stopped and looked up, so the moon lit his face.

She gasped. "You."

"Yeah."

"I don't know how to feel about this," she said, and he couldn't help but laugh. He was in complete agreement. He had come to the beach to get her off his mind, and here she was in the flesh and just as beautiful as when he left her asleep in California.

Before he lost his nerve, he blurted, "I tried to call your room when I got back to the hotel the other day. You were already gone."

"I was there for a job, and my time was up."

"And here?"

"Same. I'm here through the weekend from what I was told today."

"Oh, that's cool. I don't have a napkin here, but you're welcome to invite me to your room."

"Oh really?" She asked coolly, one brow raised.

"Yes. Unless you had other plans. And if you did, you should change them."

She made a sound much like a snort. He couldn't quite see her face in the shadow, but he could hear her breathing change.

"I had planned to take a walk along the water. I needed some fresh air, so I had not planned to go back inside just yet."

He smirked. She hadn't told him no, and she hadn't told him to get lost.

They walked together in silence for a short while before she turned and walked back toward the hotel. He followed her. He wasn't used to letting someone else lead, but he would let her have this moment. If she invited him in, he would take back control. On the way up the path, she tripped on a mound of sand, and he managed to catch her around her waist before she fell. He pulled her tight against his body, telling himself it was to make sure she had her footing before he let go, but then he didn't let go. Instead, his right hand slid up her torso, caressing her abdomen and up between her breasts. His dick

74

registered her lack of bra before his brain did. He groaned into her hair, and she leaned her head back against his chest. That was all the invitation he needed. He pulled her closer to the dunes, out of view of the hotel and further into the shadows.

CHAPTER 14
SHAR

She was restrained by his arms, barely able to move, not that she had any desire to get away. He walked right out of her dream, or maybe he walked into it. His hand continued its path up her sternum until it slid around her neck. Her heartbeat quickened, and her breaths became ragged. He used his thumb and forefinger to tilt her head to the side. She shook her head a bit, moving her hair off her shoulder. He put his lips to her skin, and she moaned. His scent enveloped her, and heat pooled between her legs. He ran his tongue up from her shoulder into the crease of her neck and to her ear where he lightly bit her lobe. When his hand tightened around her throat, she swallowed hard. She didn't believe he would hurt her, though there were things she'd like him to do. She wanted him to turn her ass pink with his hand. She wanted to choke on his cock. She really just wanted to know this wasn't a fever dream brought on by the frustration of nearly having made a big mistake with Henri.

No sooner had wetness begun to seep from her body, he tightened the grip holding her against his chest. He then slid his left hand from her waist down across her hip. She squirmed, her body thrumming with need. She rubbed against his cock, feeling his hardness through their clothes, and he groaned. When his hand got to her thigh, he hiked up the sundress she was wearing. He squeezed her inner thigh just hard enough to make her squeak, though she'd tried to hold it in. She wanted him to move his hand up, and when he finally did, she sighed in relief.

He, on the other hand, growled against her hair when he slid his hand up and grazed her naked pussy. "Oh, what a pleasant surprise," he said, and she smiled.

Normally, she would not have just wandered around with no underclothes, but it was already late, the dinner crowd was gone from the hotel's restaurant, and it was dark. She hadn't expected to come across anyone, especially not anyone she'd let get close enough to find out. When he pulled her legs apart to give him better access to her wet pussy, she had no regrets about her wardrobe choice.

"Fuck," he said through gritted teeth when his fingers slid between her lips. "You're already so fucking wet. I have half a mind to bend you over and fuck you right here where anyone could walk up on us."

She opened her mouth, but instead of the protest she was trying to form, a moan escaped her. She couldn't even deny that she would have let him take her right there. He was pushing her toward the edge with his thumb making circles on her clit and his fingers sliding in and out of her slit.

"I want you to come for me, Pretty." He removed his hand from her throat, letting her breathe freely, and he grabbed her breast tightly, using his thumb and forefinger to work her nipple into a tight pebble that just amplified the pleasure he was giving her.

"Don't stop. Please don't stop," she panted out. She was so close.

Suddenly, voices came from the direction of the hotel. Shar froze, but he didn't stop. She wiggled, thinking he'd let her go, but he didn't. Instead, his hand slid back up around her throat while his other hand kept moving in her pussy.

"Shhhh, Pretty. They'll hear you. I bet you can come before they catch us."

With adrenaline pumping through her veins and arousal firing in every nerve ending in her body, Shar was on the brink before he even finished the words.

"That's it. I feel you tightening around my fingers. You wish it was my cock, don't you. Would you like to get caught with my cock slamming in and out of you?"

That was all it took. She fell apart in his arms, small whimpers escaping as her walls clenched around his fingers. He held her up until she could control her muscles again. She whined when he pulled his fingers from her and let her dress fall. He slid his fingers into her mouth before she could make any more noise, and they both listened to the voices coming closer.

He leaned down and whispered in her ear, "I'm going to walk you to the door. Just smile and nod when whoever it is passes by us."

He let her go completely and then grabbed her hand. He led them out of the shadows and toward the center of the path. As soon as they made the first curve, they nearly walked into two teenage boys who were sneaking away from the hotel with a couple of small bottles in their hands. She noted the bottles were probably wine coolers and nothing too concerning. The boys jumped when they realized two adults were on the path, but she just smiled in their direction. True to his word, the man walked her to the door of the hotel and waited until she let herself into the building before he said goodnight.

"You're not coming in?"

She thought for sure he would come inside, so she could make sure he got off too. He shook his head and turned on his heel, heading back down the path toward the ocean.

CHAPTER 15
MACK

Mack found the teenagers about 50 yards from the path, sitting in the sand enjoying their coolers. He joined them, and they both stiffened when he sat with his feet between them.

"Let me guess," he said, his face deadpan, "family vacation, and at least one of you had to spend the day watching younger siblings." When neither of them responded, he tried again. "No? Hmmm, you got left with an older sibling and waited for them to fall asleep before you snuck out with a couple of your parents' coolers?" He purposely strengthened the inflection at the end of his question trying to get a response from them.

"What do you want, Mister?" one of them asked. He seemed to be the more defiant of the two, as the other looked like he wanted to walk into the ocean and never come out.

"Nothing, actually. I saw you two sneaking off with alcohol and wanted to make sure you were alright before I head home."

"Why didn't you stay with the lady?" the quieter one asked.

Now they were getting somewhere. The real reason Mack

had come out behind them instead of following the woman to her suite was because he wanted to make sure these kids hadn't seen or heard anything. If she was going to be staying in this hotel for a few days, he didn't want anyone making that time hell for her because they'd gotten caught by a couple of kids.

"Maybe she didn't want him to stay," the first one said. "She looked tired and probably didn't want to be bothered."

"Well, they were holding hands."

Mack chuckled at their little mystery-solver antics. That was the answer he was hoping for. They hadn't heard anything.

"We were holding hands, and she was tired. If you must know, I have to go to work early in the morning, so after our walk, I left her at the door and am going home. I just stopped to check on you two. Since you are obviously okay, I'll say goodnight."

When Mack walked into the office the next morning, he felt much lighter than he had upon his return from California. Getting to see, touch, and hear the woman's orgasm again, had him in a great mood.

"Good morning, Janet," he said on his way to his office. "Let's catch up in about fifteen if that works for you."

"I'll gather my notes and calendar, Mr. Mackenzie."

He turned on the computer and waited for it to load. Though their equipment was state of the art, it still took a long time to boot when he'd been gone for days. They hadn't yet gotten into AI, but he could almost imagine that the computer was punishing him for being away so long. Hell, it spent more time with it than with any lover who might feel the same.

While he waited, he watched the harbor. Maybe it was time for him to buy a boat. He'd never owned one before, never even thought about it, but watching them travel the narrow strip of water this morning had him imagining a boat trip up and down the coast. Then he imagined a woman on the bow with dark blonde hair blowing in the wind. A knock on the open door pulled him from the daydream.

"I can come back if you're not ready yet."

"That won't be necessary, Janet. I'm good. Just lost track of time while waiting for this computer to boot."

"Maybe it's time for a new one. Just because your office is rustic doesn't mean your technology has to match."

"What do you mean? We upgraded everything just a couple years ago."

Janet shook her head and sat in the chair opposite his desk. "No. You upgraded the rest of the company but refused to let anyone in your office saying that your computer was perfect for your needs, and you didn't want to fix what wasn't broken."

Mack's mouth dropped open. Now that she'd said it, he vaguely remembered something like that leaving his lips. He visibly cringed, and the corners of her lips pulled up. She tried to keep her face neutral, but she was failing.

"I can be an idiot sometimes, huh?"

"Occasionally," she agreed. "But you are also brilliant, empathetic, and generous. You just sometimes get ideas in your head, and you can't see past them. You forget that people exist when you're focused, and..."

"Whoa! Okay, wait. This wasn't a meeting to list all of my flaws. Damn!"

Janet gave him a full smile and then pursed her lips back into serious mode. "I am here to discuss whatever you would like."

For the next thirty minutes, she related everything that had happened in his absence, up to and including Kevin's meeting with the models who would star in their marketing campaigns. "She is quite beautiful, and I was glad to see she wasn't a stereotypical, petite model," Janet said. "And that man is handsome enough with his fake French accent, but he seems almost too old to be her partner. Not that you asked my opinion, but he looks much older than even you. He's probably older than Kevin looks."

Mack's lips quivered as he held in a laugh. Poor Kevin got the short end of the gene-pool stick. Though she'd had a hard life, his mother had been stunning. Unfortunately, Kevin inherited his father's looks, which included early hair loss and middle-age spread. Still, he'd managed to find love, and Tabitha did love him. Mack remembered the look in her eyes when she took Kevin's hand at the end of the aisle. She only had eyes for him, and Mack couldn't be happier for his dearest friend.

"Janet, let's not talk about Kevin's aging. I hear what you're saying about the male model, but it won't make things better to hurt Kevin's feelings."

"Hurt Kevin's feelings how?" came a voice from the doorway.

"I should have locked the elevator," Mack quipped with a smile at his business partner. "How was the show."

"The show was great, and my wife was happy. As for the elevator, you do remember that I have a key too, right?"

Mack laughed at his friend. Of course, he knew that the elevator being locked wouldn't deter him.

"So, how did you plan to hurt my feelings?"

Janet looked at the ground as Mack's eyes bore into her.

"If it was something Janet said, I'm sure it had to do with my hairline. Momma J has been trying to get me to shave my head bald for months now. Nope, too many knocks on this noggin for that to even look good." Kevin winked at Janet and chuckled. "Now for the important stuff. I already reached out to the models and asked them to hang around through

Monday. Janet, if you could extend their hotel stays, drivers, and reschedule their flights, please. We'll be good to go on that end."

"Sounds good. When we finish here, I will reach out to the Board members and try to get the majority here Monday morning," Mack offered.

"Already done," Kevin said with a smirk. "You obviously haven't checked your email yet this morning."

Mack sighed. "No, I was actually just discussing my need for an upgraded system."

Kevin looked at Janet who shrugged. "It's about time," was all he said.

The phone rang in the foyer, and Janet looked in Mack's direction. "I believe that's all for now, Janet," Mack said, and she was gone from the room.

"Don't even say what you're thinking," Kevin blurted. "We just gave her a raise, the second in six months."

Mack laughed and then turned serious. "How in the hell did we get anything done before she showed up to keep us in line?"

"I have no fucking idea, but you will not get me to say that aloud with her in the room," Kevin tried to maintain a straight face, but the corners of his mouth quirked up making Mack laugh again.

Rather than fight with his old desktop, Mack pulled out his tablet. At least that was updated. He moved to the small conference table near the corner of the office and gestured for Kevin to join him. Kevin pulled out his phone, and Mack had to remind himself to upgrade his phone to the Version 2. If Kevin was able to use it in lieu of his laptop, it would be worth having.

For the next few hours, the men poured over the marketing plan for the Version 2, as well as some additional marketing for their service plans. Kevin had found some technology conferences where they could present their new products. At least one of the models, likely the woman, would be invited to attend as well since they planned for her to be the face of the phone line. They slowly built out a calendar of events and photo ops. The goal was to have more specifics to share with the models, the photographer and the videographer, and also the Board of Directors on Monday.

"Did you invite the agents as well?" Mack asked.

"Yes. Thus far, everyone has said yes. I'm just waiting to hear back from two of the Board members and the male model's agent."

"Janet didn't seem to think too highly of that guy."

Kevin raised a brow.

"That's what we were talking about when you arrived. She said he looked too old for the woman, and she didn't like his fake French accent."

"Did she really say his accent was fake?" He started laughing and then choked on his own spit. Mack quickly passed him a bottle of water from the mini fridge.

"Breathe, man. You can't die in my office. Someone will think I offed my partner to gain 100% control of the company."

Once he'd gotten his breathing and coughing under control again, Kevin responded. "You watch too much damn true crime."

"Probably, but I love it."

"Speaking of love," Kevin said, staring intently at Mack's face. "How'd you sleep last night?"

"Like a dream." Mack smiled at the memory of his hands and mouth on her. The possibility of getting caught had only heightened his desire to make her come. If not for the looks on the boys' faces, he probably would not have made it to work on time this morning because he would have joined her in her suite. He was looking forward to trying to find her tonight when he left the office. A few waves first, and then he'd ride her.

"Hey, Mack, buddy, where'd you go?" Kevin waved his hand in front of Mack's face.

"Oh, sorry. I was thinking about riding some waves this afternoon.

"Damn, whatever you did to release some of your tension last night must've really worked."

"Oh yeah, like a dream."

Kevin smiled and made his way toward the door. "I'll get all of our notes put into some sort of agenda for Monday, and we can go over it again tomorrow with fresh eyes."

"Sounds good."

As soon as Kevin was out the door, Janet came over the intercom. "Mr. Mackenzie, technology will be here around lunch to change out your system. If there's anything important on your desktop that isn't in the cloud, go ahead and get those files downloaded or else uploaded to the cloud before lunch."

"That quick, huh?"

"Yes. It's easy to make happen when the boss calls."

"Thanks, Janet," Mack said absentmindedly. He looked at the computer and thought about the file he'd haphazardly saved in different places rather than in the cloud. Shit, it was going to take him the rest of the morning to get them all moved to a safe place, especially if the computer was still working as slowly as it had been earlier when he'd first turned it on. Then, he'd have to get the new one set up to his liking. Now, he remembered why he wouldn't let anyone touch his computer during the last company-wide system upgrade they had. "Fuck me," he said aloud to the empty office.

Mack had been correct in his calculations. Jason from the tech department walked into the office not minutes after Mack had transferred the last of his needed files to the cloud. Rather than order lunch to pass the time, Mack decided to take a walk along the harbor, letting Jason work in peace. The entire process wasn't supposed to take much longer than an hour. Not only were they going to change out all of the physical components, but they would also update all of the apps he regularly used to the most recent versions. According to Jason, that is the part that would take the longest. Before he left, Mack wrote a list of the programs he used most often and a few he wanted to try.

The harbor was surprisingly quiet for a random Wednesday early in the season. He expected to see more personal boats trying to moor at the public docks, but there were plenty of empty slips still. He was also ready for a long wait at his favorite fish and chips spot, but the place was relatively empty.

"Mack." Charlie the shop owner called out to him. "I haven't seen you in months. Where've you been?"

"Busy. I rarely get a chance to leave the office during the day unless I have a meeting. Usually, I get my assistant to order my lunch and have it delivered, or else she comes and picks it up."

"Yes, I know Janet well. She's a lovely woman, a fine woman."

A smile played on Mack's lips. "You're not out here flirting with my assistant, are you, Charlie?"

"Hell yes, I'm flirting. I would take that woman home to meet my mother if she were still alive. I'm old, but I'm not dead."

Mack laughed at Charlie's response. He wondered whether Janet had any reciprocal feelings for Charlie. Maybe he could play matchmaker. Maybe having someone else to fuss over would keep her out of Mack's business or from fussing over Kevin's hairline.

"Let me get an order to go, my friend."

"Sure thing. Let me make some fresh. I can't have you going back to the office and telling Janet that I gave you food that had been sitting under the heat lamps. She wouldn't take too kindly to that." He pulled freshly battered filets out of the refrigerator as he mused about Janet's possible responses. "Though," he said, ruminating to himself," she might feel the need to come down here and yell at me herself. I bet she's beautiful riled up." Just then, he looked up at Mack like he was awaiting confirmation. There was no way Mack was going to provide a response. He did not think Janet was beautiful when she was reprimanding him for something.

To further punctuate his refusal to answer, Mack turned back toward the harbor while he waited for his food. It really was a beautiful day. He'd bet the woman was lounging on a chaise behind her hotel watching the waves or maybe she was reading a book. He remembered that she'd had a book of sorts with her when they'd first met in California. What strange coincidence had them once again in the same place on the other side of the country? He didn't believe in fate, so he couldn't even consider that possibility, but damn if it didn't feel like something was working in his favor. Last night was like payback for the time and embarrassment from all that had happened in Cali after he'd left her asleep that morning.

Before he knew it, Charlie was calling his name, and he was heading back toward the office. Of course, he couldn't walk away without ribbing the old guy just a bit. "Thanks, Charlie. I'll be sure to tell Janet that you want to see her angry. Better yet, the next time she gets mad at me or Kevin, I'll just send her this way." Charlie laughed, and Mack waved to the old man as he walked away.

"Technology just finished setting up your office about ten minutes ago. They said to call them if something isn't to your liking." When Mack smiled at her, Janet's brows furrowed. "Why are you looking at me like that?"

"No reason," he said, knowing she would not believe the lie.

"Sloan Mackenzie, you know you are not a good liar."

He broke out in a wide grin and offered her some of his lunch. When she saw what he had brought, her cheeks developed a pinkish hue, at least as much as her medium brown skin would allow.

"Interesting," he said with a tilt of his head.

"What?" Her voice took on a shrill tone, that simple word more of an accusation than a question.

"I had a very nice walk along the harbor, and I was so glad Charlie had the fish and chips shop open when I got there. He, um, how should I put this?"

"You shouldn't," she said with a matter-of-fact tone. "You should mind your business, Mr. Mackenzie."

"I am, Momma J."

CHAPTER 16

SHAR

S har woke herself with a moan. She had been having the most erotic dream of her unnamed surfer riding the waves of her orgasm. Her hands were locked between her thighs, and her clit was swollen. She rarely slept naked when she was alone, which was most nights, so the unexpected release had her trembling. There was something about that man that made her libido fly off the rails. It wasn't just her normal get-and-give, one-night stand, especially not since they'd seen each other again. She wanted to see more of him. Hell, she wanted him. The fact that he left after she'd all but invited him in last night should have pissed her off enough to forget about him, but it made her more anxious to see what would happen the next time they met. What in the hell was he doing here anyway? Before she could posit possible reasons, her phone rang.

"Jerry, it's barely 8am. Why are you calling me? Is the world ending?"

"No, sleeping beauty. I wanted to make sure you'd been informed about the change in your itinerary."

"If you mean about staying through Monday, yes. Kevin called me yesterday evening."

"Okay, good. I had hoped so, but I wanted to make sure before I started working on some other things."

"Other things?"

"Yes, my dear. You do know I have other clients, right?"

She groaned. "You and I both know that I was your first and remain your favorite."

"We do, but my other clients do not."

"You cheating bastard!"

Jerry laughed. "Better to cheat on you and get paid than to cheat on Geoffrey."

"Okay, that's fair. How is my husband twice removed?"

"Just as lazy as you. I bet you two were doing the same thing right before I called."

Now it was her turn to laugh. "Oh, I doubt that," she said while sitting up against the pillows. "Ugh, why are hotel pillows always so soft?"

"If you'd keep a man, you could just use him as a pillow."

"That was low, even for you."

"To the window, to the wall, baby! Now tell me what has you so riled up this morning, or should I ask who?"

Shar climbed out of the bed and put the phone on speaker, so she could set it on the sink. "Do you remember how I told you we needed to chat about this guy I met in California?"

"Yes," he said, his voice taking on an excited tone. "We were supposed to meet for dinner this Saturday, so you could dish."

"Yeah, well, he's here now."

"What!"

She could picture Jerry jumping up from his seat. If they had been together, he'd be congratulating her on the engagement. She shook her head and smiled.

"It's not like that. Actually, I'm not sure what it's like really."

"What do you mean? He's not a stalker, is he?"

"No." Though she said it emphatically, she couldn't help

the moment of uncertainty now that Jerry said the word. "At least, I don't think so."

"So, fate brought you two together again?"

"Are you going to let me pour the tea, or do you want to brew your own this morning?"

Just then, Geoffrey's voice came through the phone. "Good morning, beautiful. I knew my wayward husband was talking to you with all that screaming he just did."

"Your wayward husband just told me he's cheating on me with other clients. Something about needing to make money."

"Well, you know I do like to be a kept man. Anyway, is everything good where you are? The way he yelled, I got worried and came downstairs to check."

"I'm good. He was just making up stories about my sex life rather than listening to me."

"Haha, that's because your stories always end the same way. You send them home brokenhearted and alone with flaccid, well-worn dicks."

"I send them home satisfied," she retorted. "Now, do you two want to hear my story or what? I haven't had breakfast yet, so you don't have a lot of time."

While her favorite couple got their shit together and cups of coffee were prepared, she grabbed her phone and headed to the small kitchenette to grab herself a bottle of water. They were going to want all the details, so she'd need something to keep her hydrated. She giggled to herself again thinking about the surfer. Fuck, he could dehydrate her without argument.

"What are you laughing at?"

"You two arguing over coffee instead of sitting down to hear this juicy gossip."

"Oh, we're ready now. Seated and set. Go!"

She smiled and took a seat on the stool that looked out toward the balcony. "So, when I was at my last stop in California before that shoot at the art gallery, I saw this sexy ass surfer. I thought he was a young one and almost ignored him completely, but something about him caught my attention and wouldn't let go. The second day, I sent him a note to meet me at my room, and he did. He was not young, and the experience he gave me had me unable to walk by the morning."

"Hold up, he outlasted you?" Geoffrey asked.

"You let him stay long enough to make your knees weak?" Jerry added to the question.

"He manhandled me in all the right ways." A gasp came from the other side of the phone. "Seriously, this man choked me first with his hand and then with his cock. I couldn't even think straight."

"Damn!" they both said in unison.

"I know, right? I don't even want a man smacking my ass half the time because it makes them think they run shit. The thing is, I'd have let that man do whatever the fuck he wanted."

She paused the story expecting one of the men to say something, but they were both silent. She looked at her phone afraid the connection had failed and then laughed. "You two are never this quiet."

"Girl, we are enthralled, do you hear me. Don't stop now."

"Question," Jerry finally said. "Did you get his name?"

She sighed. "No, and I fucking regret it. But the story is not over. There's still more to tell, and then there are some things I need to tell you in confidence as my agent and not my friend just in case something comes of it later."

"Just let me know when the good stuff is over, and I'll take my happy ass back to bed."

"Thanks, Geoffrey."

"Ok, so back to the story. No, I did not get his name. I did not expect to think about him again once he left my room. I got up, checked out of the hotel, and went to the photoshoot. I was supposed to head home right after that, remember?"

"Right. Makes sense," Jerry admitted.

She thought again about what strange coincidence brought them together here in the dark on a random stretch of beach on the opposite coast. It made no sense, but she wouldn't be upset about it.

"So, I get here with plans to hook up with someone I saw on the plane."

"Damn, you work quick," Geoffrey said with a laugh.

"You already know, my friend. You already know. Anyway, that plan fell through, so I came back to my hotel, which is absolutely perfect, Jerry, thanks! The sun had already set by the time I got here, but I wanted to go out and stick my feet in the water. I made it down the path, and as soon as I come out of the dunes, I damn near run into this guy. I couldn't see him because of the dunes and the dark. He grabs a hold of me to keep us both from falling over and then says he recognizes me."

"Oh hell no. He's a stalker, girl. Let me call Velocity in the morning and get you the hell out of there."

"Calm down, killer. He was just as shocked as I was when I got to see his face in the moonlight. There was no way he could have known where I was, that I was coming here, or what hotel I'd be at." When Jerry didn't interject anything else, she continued. "We took a wonderfully serene walk along the water together. No, we didn't really talk, nor did we exchange names. We just kept each other company. Then he walked me back to the hotel."

"That's it? Are you telling me, I got out of bed for a simple 'he walked me back to the hotel?'"

She burst out laughing at his mocking tone. "If 'he walked me back to the hotel' had an air of he pulled me into the shadows and fingered me while his hand wrapped around my throat until I came right before we were caught by two kids sneaking out with their parents wine coolers, then yes, he simply walked me back to the hotel."

"Holy shit, girl. You just let that dude get you off in public? That's bold, even for you."

"I told you I'd let him do just about anything he wanted. All he had to do was touch me, and I was dripping wet."

"So, you made plans to see him again, right?"

"Um...that's part of the problem." She stepped out onto the balcony to hear the waves while they grilled her with questions she didn't want to answer. "I thought he was going to come up to the room last night, but he just dropped me at the door of the hotel."

"Wait, he got you off and then left. He didn't even ask you to reciprocate."

She saw a few surfboards out on the water and found herself staring hard to see if one of them looked familiar. They all looked like kids. No one that resembled her surfer. She fought hard to tamp down the disappointment that wanted to rise in her chest.

"No, he simply told me goodnight and turned to leave."

"Did you get his name this time?"

"Nope. Like I said, we didn't talk much."

"Girl, I am so disappointed. I thought we were going to be hearing wedding bells, or at least ass clapping." Geoffrey said before adding, "I'm going back upstairs now."

"I believe I will see him again. I do, but there was no plan made. You know I'll let you know if anything changes."

The call went silent for a few moments, and then shifting sounds came through the speaker. "Okay, my dear, I'm in my office with the door closed. What do you need me to know."

Shar sighed. She really wished she didn't have to tell Jerry about the situation with Henri, but it was necessary to cover herself should any issues arise later. She took a deep breath and then explained the conversation on the flight, the dinner, and the plans to go back to Henri's hotel. She didn't go into details about everything that was said, but she made sure he understood that Henri was serious about wanting her.

"How did you find out that you were working together on the Velocity campaigns?"

"I asked about the meeting he claimed to have that next morning, and he told me. I nearly had a panic attack and had to excuse myself to the restroom for a few moments. I wish I would have known earlier."

"I'm sorry," Jerry said quietly.

Shar had been leaning on the railing watching the surfers, but she stood and reentered the suite, closing the sliding door behind her. "Sorry for what, Jer?" It was so rare that her friend quietly apologized that she knew he felt responsible for at least part of what had happened.

"I didn't know for sure that Henri would be your partner in the campaigns, but I did give his name as a suggestion."

"What do you mean?" she asked, her voice coming out as a screech.

"When I was in negotiations with Kevin Dulaney, he asked me if I had any suggestions for male models you've worked with before. He wanted someone with whom you seemed to have good chemistry on camera." Jerry took a deep breath, and Shar's stomach tightened. "You two looked so good together during that canyon shoot that I told Kevin to reach out to Henri's agent. I even gave him the phone number to call."

"Shit, Jerry, really? You know, sometimes, I wish you would let me in on some of the stuff that is happening while it's happening." She pulled out the stool next to the kitchen island and sat in it. "Truth be told, though, I would have likely agreed with you then. The shoot was a lot of fun, and the final photos were awesome. I also didn't know he was remotely interested in me until we were on the plane coming here."

"Still," Jerry began, remorse in his voice, "If you had known his name had been put in as a recommendation, you could have nipped the potential hookup in the bud rather than after the foreplay had started."

"Right. Like I said, though, I don't think anything will come of it. I just wanted to give you a head's up."

"Okay. Let's talk more after the meeting Monday morning. We can do lunch before our flights out."

"You'll be here?" Her voice was much livelier than it had been for the past thirty minutes.

"Yes, agents were invited as well."

"Okay, great! See you then," Shar said, ending the call before they could bring up anything else.

She was exhausted from that long phone call. She'd never been a fan of talking on the phone, even when she loved the person she was talking to. Texting was much more her speed. In fact, Jerry and Geoffrey were probably the only people she had had an actual phone conversation with in the past five years. Maybe she needed to make more friends. No sooner had the thought popped into her head than she dismissed it. She didn't have the time for friends, nor did she want to go through the process of meeting new people outside of work. That thought made her heart race and her palms sweat. Nope, she was perfectly happy with her two best friends.

By the end of the week, Shar was antsy. She hadn't seen the hot surfer since the other night in the dunes. Her pussy tightened just thinking about the way he made her come in public with the impending likelihood of being seen. There was no way he hadn't enjoyed himself, so why hadn't she seen him? Why hadn't he come back to the hotel to look for her or even showed up at this end of the beach to surf. It's like he disappeared. She didn't want to think that maybe he had decided to reciprocate her disappearing act. He didn't seem the petty type, but she was only here for another couple days, and she needed to get laid.

She scanned the beach, as she had done every day, and her eyes landed on a group of surfers waiting for the perfect wave. Their heads bobbed up and down amidst the undulating waves, and her hopes rose when she noticed a head of wavy blond hair in the group. Was he finally back? Half of the men began paddling toward the shore, moving to stand on their boards, and she pulled her sunglasses back down to cover how intently she was staring in their direction. They looked like their own wave of perfectly formed bodies, and any other day, she'd have been calculating how many of them she could have before the weekend was over. Today, however, her eyes locked onto one rider, and the rest of the crowd, on the beach and in the water, melted away.

His movements were like silk. They were similar to the way he fucked—smooth control. He didn't falter once, not even an ill-timed tremble. He was perfection in the water, and in bed, and she wanted him again. This time, she planned to take control...if she could just get his damn attention.

The men hit the sand and picked up their boards, heading in toward the hotel bar. She pulled her glasses down to make it more obvious she was watching, but he never turned his head. Dammit! What game was he playing? Did he expect her to come to him? That wasn't her style. She turned back toward the waves.

A voice spoke close enough to her ear that she could feel his breath, and her insides turned to mush. "You should learn to go after what you want, Pretty, not just watch it walk by."

"Is that what you do?" She kept herself from looking in his direction, though her entire body was consumed by his nearness.

"Always."

Her spine stiffened at that tiny word. What did that mean if he hadn't sought her out all week. Did that mean he didn't want her? Had he gotten all he wanted? Shit! She knew this was no love match and never intended it to be more than a fun fling, but damn, she didn't expect to be dismissed so quickly. She'd never been dismissed so quickly. She felt, more than heard, him walk away, and she was suddenly cold, though the sun beamed down. Gathering her coverup and beach bag, she headed inside to her room for a hot shower and to find something else to distract her from the thoughts swirling through her mind. There was no way in hell she was letting some random guy make her feel insecure.

CHAPTER 17

SHAR

The shower did nothing to improve Shar's mood. The silkiness of the suds running over her breasts and down between her thighs had her hornier and more frustrated than she was when he left her sitting on the beach. Fuck him! There were plenty of other men around to take care of her needs.

Hair pulled back into a chic bun, she looked at herself in the mirror and dropped her towel to the floor. She pulled on one of her slinkiest cocktail dresses, letting the fabric slide over her skin like liquid silver, the chain-like straps clinking against her earrings as they fell into place. The cool color was a striking contrast against her tanned skin, and it fell just low enough to cover her thong. She finished the look off with black stilettos and a black clutch. She was not ending the night alone.

Her first stop was the bar by the lobby. Time to pre-game with a couple of tequila shots before heading to the clubs down the strip. It barely took fifteen minutes before men began approaching, asking her name, and offering to buy her a drink. Most of them were much older, even older than the surfer who would not get out of her head, so she smiled and then ignored them. She was looking for different energy tonight.

"Where's the party?" A melodious voice came from her left.

Though she was getting ready to leave, she gave him a once over and decided that he might be worth delaying her departure for a few minutes. She licked her lips and took the final sip of her drink. "I heard there's a couple of fun spots down the strip. I thought I'd hit them up and see what's happening."

His dark eyes took her in slowly from head to toe before he invited her to join him and his friends as they bar hopped the strip. Apparently, it was a wedding weekend, and he was the only one there without a significant other. Or at least that was his story. She didn't believe him for a heartbeat, and for all she knew, he was the groom-to-be, but she also didn't care. He looked safe and like he'd be fun for the night. That was all she wanted.

Though she had planned to grab a cab to the furthest spot on the strip and work her way back toward her hotel, the group had decided to go the other direction. It was inconvenient, but she wasn't bothered. So long as she didn't end the night alone, a longer ride there or back would not matter. His group consisted of three other couples who all looked like they were barely out of college. She didn't bother learning anyone's name because she had no intentions of seeing any of them again after tonight.

"So do you live here?" one of the guys asked, his date clinging to his arm like she was either too drunk to stand already or she was afraid he would disappear should she let him go.

"No, I'm just here for the weekend." She wasn't going to tell them that she was here for work because then they would want more details. They always wanted more details. The only person who hadn't wanted more details left her sitting alone and frustrated on a lounge chair this afternoon. She shook her head to clear those thoughts, grabbed her drink from the bar, a Long Island this time, and made her way to the dance floor. She was going to get that man out of her head.

"Do you mind if I join you?" her dark-eyed date asked, grabbing her around the waist. She put her arms around his neck, making sure not to spill any of her drink on his shirt. He pulled her tight against his torso, and as they moved to the music, she felt the stirrings of his arousal. It wasn't going to be a life-changing night, but it'd do.

By the time they got to the second bar, most of the girls in their group, were pissy drunk, each taking on a different persona. There was the complainer who just wanted to go back to the hotel, a crier, and the horny bitch whose date spent most of the night trying to keep her hands out of his pants. He should've just taken her in the bathroom and gotten it out of her system. Shar couldn't help but think that they'd all have been much happier.

At the last bar, Shar and her date were the only ones left, and he kept throwing hints that they head to his hotel room. The longer they had spent together with his friends, and the more he drank, the less interested she was in spending the night with him. When he went to the bathroom for the fourth time, she considered hailing a cab, but she felt guilty since he was still out alone because of her. So, she turned to the bartender, and ordered herself a soda. One of them needed to drink less.

"What are you doing at this end of the strip, Pretty?"

Her breath caught, as that silky smooth voice washed over her. She tried to ignore him, but his hand was on her bare hip, her dress having crept up as she sat on the barstool. She felt the roughness of his hands kneading the flesh of her upper thigh, and her panties were instantly drenched. My god, he had some kind of spell over her body. The bartender set her drink down and looked between the two of them. His knitted brows drew her out of the trance this man's hands were weaving around her.

She turned to face him. "I'm here with my date."

He smirked. "Oh really, and where is this date of yours?"

"In the restroom, if you must know. We were getting ready to head back to the hotel."

A darkness crept across his face before he blinked it away and laughed, looking at the new drink she had just ordered. Still, he nodded in acquiescence and walked away, blending into the crowd around the dance floor. Goosebumps formed on her bare arms and legs, as if he had taken all of her heat with him, like maybe he was heat itself.

"Sorry, I took so long," her nearly forgotten date said, leaning on the bar beside her. His words were slurring, and his lean was probably more from necessity than charm. She had started the night sure she would end it getting all her needs met, but she had no desire to take advantage of a drunk kid who suddenly made her feel old at her professional age of twenty-three, let alone her real age of twenty-six.

"Thank you for a very nice time. It was great to meet you and your friends, but I think it's time I get some sleep."

"What do you mean? The night is young, and so are we." He grabbed her arm and spun the stool around, so she was facing him. He placed his knee between her thighs before she realized what was happening. His face was inches away from hers, and his hand was running up her thigh.

"What are you doing?" She tried to push his hand away and turn herself, so she was at least facing the bar directly, but he held her in place, his knee brushing her panties.

"Look at you, wet for me already." His hand squeezed her thigh until she squealed, and he laughed. "I bet you like it rough, don't you." She was shaking her head. This could not be happening in a busy bar, at the bar, with all these people around.

"Let me go." She said it as directly as she could while

trying not to draw too much attention, but he closed the distance, trying to kiss her. She turned her head just in time, so his tongue grazed her chin instead, and she recoiled. His breath was putrid, as if he had just vomited in the bathroom. She put her hands up to push him away, but he was stronger than her, even in his drunken state, and he pushed her back into the seat, her arm bumping the guy on the stool next to her. Why hadn't they left when his friends had? Why hadn't she left when he was in the bathroom?

Finally, the person sitting next to her turned around and shouted, "What the hell, dude?"

He looked up at him with a sneer. "Mind your bus..." His sneer turned to a whimper, as a hand came from behind Shar and clamped onto his wrist, bending his hand back.

"I suggest you remove your other hand from her before I remove it completely." There was venom in the tone, but she'd have recognized that voice anywhere.

The guy slowly lifted his right hand from her thigh. "Get off of me," Shar yelled, trying to push his knee from between her legs. She didn't have to push hard because her surfer turned her stool slightly and dragged the guy away from her and onto the floor. He was crying at this point from the pressure of his wrist still being twisted in an awkward position.

"Please. Please. I'm sorry. I didn't mean anything by it. I thought she was into it."

"When a woman tells you to let her go, turns away from you, and pushes you away, you listen, you little prick." He dragged the kid outside and put him in a taxi. She was glad she could see them through the window because she was afraid he was going to do much worse. She watched for the surfer to come back into the bar while a group of women gathered around asking if she was okay. She was not okay.

"Are you ready to leave now, Pretty?" His voice was little more than a whisper in her ear. She nodded silently and grabbed her bag from the bar. She put her arms around his waist and let him lead her outside.

"It's Shar," she said quietly. When he didn't respond, she repeated, "My name is Shar, not Pretty."

He led her to a black sports car that was parked outside the bar. His finger under her chin, he lifted her face to look at him. "I call you pretty because you are, and I like the way you respond when I say it. Now you're shaking, so let's get you warmed up." He opened the car door and let her in before he climbed in behind the wheel on the other side.

CHAPTER 18

MACK

Mack wanted to kick himself. He shouldn't have just walked away from her when he came out of the water this afternoon. He knew he was trying to push her buttons, but he just couldn't help himself. He liked when she was riled. She was beautiful when she thought she was in control, but damn, his dick ached when things weren't going her way. Still, he should've told her he was just going to shower and change. She'd have waited for him. He knew she would have. As soon as he pulled back into the parking lot, though, she was getting in a fucking cab with that young fuck.

He hadn't even bothered getting out of his car, just followed the cab. He considered going home, but he wanted to see how things would play out. The way she responded to him didn't make him think she was the type of woman to just flow with a crowd. He'd watched the group getting drunk and withering away little by little. He wondered if those other couples were actually couples or if the guys had just picked up random women around town the same way she had been plucked from the hotel. When he caught her 'date' vomiting in the bathroom, he knew the farce would be over soon, but he should have made her leave with him then. His pride just wouldn't let him. He wanted her to come to him willingly and not because of some other man's actions.

Instead, he'd left her there to damn near be accosted by that kid. It had taken every ounce of restraint not to beat him to a pulp, even in the kid's drunken state. Putting him into a cab and sending him to his hotel, whichever hotel he was staying was a gift. And now, looking over at the woman he'd been thinking about all week, he felt powerless and pissed off. She was staring out the windshield blankly, and her body was trembling. The weather had been warm, so he hadn't bothered with a jacket that he could have wrapped around her. That sexy ass dress was doing nothing to help keep her warm, as she processed what had just happened.

Without thinking, he bypassed her hotel and made his way to his house. When he opened her door, she sat there silently, and when he reached his arms around her, she looked through him like he wasn't there. Maybe she was drunker than he had thought when he talked to her for those few moments at the bar. He honestly had no idea how much or what she had been drinking all night. All he knew was that he wouldn't leave her alone tonight. He would watch over her and make sure she was all right like he had called himself doing until it really mattered.

"Fuck!" he said under his breath when he looked at himself in the mirror after tucking her into the bed under his comforter. He wasn't her father, though he knew she was much younger than himself, but he had sat there with her until she fell asleep. He knew it wasn't his job to watch over this woman. They hardly knew each other, and she hadn't asked him to follow her around tonight. Hell, he didn't even know her name until right before they got in his car, and it wasn't like he had even invited her to come home with him. "Fuck, fuck, fuck!"

He went to his liquor cabinet and poured himself a drink. After one sip, he set the cup down and crept back into his room. As quietly as he could in his irritated state, he fumbled through his dressers for some pajama bottoms. Surprisingly, he found some he'd bought for Kevin's wedding weekend. He hadn't worn them since, but he was thankful for them tonight. He didn't want her to wake up, especially not if she had any nightmares, and find him naked trying to comfort her. What comfort would that be?

Grabbing a light blanket from the closet, he made his way to the small couch in the corner of his room under the windows that overlooked the bay and curled up to sleep. He could have gone to another room, but he was afraid she'd have a nightmare and be all alone. So, he kept his vigil in the shadows but close enough in case she needed him. Tonight did not go anything like he had planned.

Mack was already awake when he saw her stirring. She opened her eyes and looked around as if trying to orient herself. When she froze, he imagined she was replaying the previous night. She must have thought she was alone because she groaned and said, "What the hell was I thinking?"

Though he didn't want to frighten her, he couldn't keep himself from responding. "I was wondering the same thing."

"I don't need your judgment this morning," she quipped. "I have enough of my own."

She sat up in the middle of the bed. Her hair was a disheveled mess, and he just watched her take herself in through the closet mirrors. She reached up and started pulling pins from her hair, letting the remnants of last night's bun fall around her shoulders. Suddenly she asked him the time.

"Just about noon."

She flopped back on the bed, and he couldn't help but chuckle. She was adorable.

"Is that all you're gonna do? Sit over there in the shadows and laugh at me?"

There was no bite to her words, but he couldn't help himself from trying to rile her. Though she seemed little worse for wear from the previous night, he was still irritated at her and himself, and now he was exhausted from hardly sleeping.

"No, that was not all I had planned for today. In fact, I had plenty of other things planned for the day besides babysitting you."

"I don't need a babysitter, okay. I am grown, and even grown folk make bad decisions sometimes."

He stood at that statement, and she sat up. "How many bad decisions have you made this week, Pretty?"

She swallowed hard when he stood in front of her. She looked him up and down, taking in his naked torso, and her eyes hovered over the waistband of his loose-fitting pajama pants. He wasn't naked, but he had gotten hot during the night and took off his shirt. The hunger in her eyes was evident, and his dick began to stir. She cleared her throat before looking into his eyes. He lifted a brow at her, still waiting for an answer.

"Why don't you tell me?" she asked defiantly. "You think you have all the answers."

"Let's see." Holding her gaze, he put his hands on the bed, so he was eye level with her. "You invited a stranger to your room and stripped naked. You didn't even know his name, nor did you ever ask. You simply let him fuck you senseless and leave without a word."

He put a knee on the bed, and she swallowed.

"Then, when you see him again on the other side of the fucking country, you don't consider how you both wound up in the same place, you just let him take control of your body again. You come on his fingers moments before you get caught, and even after that, you invite him up to your room...again. Not only that, but you stalk the beach watching for him for days. And when you finally see him, the man you'd been thinking about, you did nothing to go after him, even when he told you to. You just sat there."

She took a shuddering breath and looked down at her hands. He wasn't letting her off the hook that easily. He was hot now.

"Look at me."

Though his voice remained calm, he might as well have yelled the way her eyes snapped back up to his. He put another knee on the bed.

"You weren't done yet, though. No. You decided to join up with a frat boy and bar hop with him until he was pissy drunk. Did you leave when you had the opportunity?"

He continued stalking toward her, one hand and one knee moving at a time. She bit her lip and looked like she wanted to cry simultaneously. He wanted to strangle her for how much danger she had put herself in all week, even though he was one of the dangers. Fuck, he wanted to hurt her and protect her at the same time. He wanted to bury himself in her and just hold her. He'd never felt so compelled by a woman before. It was illogical and made him crazy.

"Now, you wake up in that same stranger's bed disoriented, and you don't try to leave. Why?"

He was mere inches from face, and his eyes bore into hers.

"I'm not afraid of you," she said.

"Maybe you should be."

He captured her mouth, pushing her back onto the bed and covering her body with his own. His control snapped, and his hands, mouth, and tongue went everywhere at once. A moan slipped, and he wasn't sure if it was hers or his own. Maybe they both moaned. He slid her barely-there dress straps off her shoulders and sucked her nipple into his mouth, grazing the sensitive tip with his teeth until her back arched.

After repeating the actions with the other nipple, he kissed his way down her stomach. When her hips lifted off the bed, he settled himself between her legs and inhaled deeply, his nose nearly pressed against her slit.

His eyes rolled back as he took in the banquet before him. Looking up into her eyes that were watching him intently, he slid his tongue between her lips, lightly caressing the tip of her clit. She clenched the sheets on either side and when she tried to lift her hips to press into his flitting tongue, his hands held her in place. He continued to tease her, letting his tongue find her hole and lapping all the way back to her clit before circling the bud faster.

As he increased the intensity of his onslaught, she threw her head back. Her moans came more frequently, and he knew she was getting closer to her release. He wrapped his lips around her clit and sucked. Her head snapped back to watch him, and he almost laughed until she begged him not to stop.

"Oh my god!" she said.

He smiled against her pussy and then lifted his head. "Not yet, Pretty."

"What?" Her question was breathy.

He licked right below her belly button and then pulled his tongue slowly back up to her sternum. He worked his way up her body until his cock, hard and ready, sat between her legs. She moaned, and he situated his face right above hers as she lifted her hips to better accommodate him.

"My name is Mack, and when you come, it'll be my name on your lips."

He slid into her effortlessly, filling her at the same time his tongue entered her mouth. She licked his lips, cleaning her juices from his face, and he moaned. Then she ran her hands around his back, sliding them down to grasp his ass like she wanted to pull him as far into her as possible. Without missing a stroke, he grabbed her hands and pulled them up above her head.

"Hold onto the headboard."

She moaned, and he picked up the pace, propping her ankles on his shoulders. She started lifting herself off the bed, using the leverage of the headboard and his body. Neither of them would be lasting much longer at this rate. At one point, she held her breath before letting out a long "Fuuuuuck."

His ego soared. "That's it, Pretty. Take what you need!"

She matched him stroke for stroke, pulling her hips up until they were both breathing heavy. Her walls tightened around him.

"Shit," he said.

"Shit, I'm gonna come," she responded, and then her body went rigid. Still, he pounded in and out of her, ensuring every inch of her walls pulsed around every inch of him. He could not get enough.

"Yes, yes, yes," she yelled like a mantra.

He released one of her hips and slid his hand up toward her throat. His breathing was ragged with the exertion and control, as he held off his own orgasm to elongate hers. She locked eyes with him, and his nostrils flared.

"Say my name," he commanded.

She stared at him, defiance in her eyes, though her hands remained locked around the top of the headboard. When he squeezed his hand at the base of her neck, though, an almost inaudible "Mack" left her lips. Then she fell apart, her hands dropping to her sides and her body seeming to melt in his hands. No sooner had she spoken his name than his own erratic breaths matched his thrusts until he arched his back and yelled his release. He collapsed on top of her, unable to move.

CHAPTER 19
MACK

They remained in bed most of the day, exploring each other's bodies until they were spent. When Shar finally admitted she was hungry, Mack went for takeout. He smiled to himself in the car as he thought about how bad in California he had wanted to take her to dinner. Who knew that not even a week later, she'd be here in his house waiting for him to bring her dinner. This had been one of the craziest weeks he'd had in years for so many reasons, not the least of which was this thing with Shar. He didn't know what to call it, but he knew it was different from his previous experiences.

He had returned to the house and set out the food on the island in his kitchen. He'd heard her turn the shower off moments after he entered through the garage. He assumed she'd found everything she needed since she hadn't exactly packed for an overnight stay. When she walked out of the bedroom in one of his white button downs, his mouth went dry, and he nearly forgot about dinner altogether.

"Why are you looking at me like that?" Shar asked, halting in the doorway.

"Because I don't think I've seen anything sexier than you

freshly showered in my shirt, especially when my mind conjures up the thought that you likely don't have anything on underneath."

She turned to the side and lifted the shirt tails to show her bare ass.

He growled, "Don't play with me, little girl," before putting down the utensils and stalking toward her.

"Ok, old man," she said with a laugh, putting her hands out and trying to dodge around him.

He reached his long arms around her waist and pulled her back against his chest. With his mouth near her ear, he asked, "Do you remember the last time I had you in this position?"

Her breaths were heavy, and not from exertion, but she said nothing.

"No answer, huh?" He slid his left hand down to her thighs, so he could lift under the shirt. He kissed in the crease of her neck and shoulder as his left hand gripped the front of his shirt. "No. Still don't remember?"

She lifted her hand and ran it through his hair, grasping it tightly to pull him back into her neck. He smiled at the gesture and nipped lightly at her skin. He dragged his nails up her thigh until he found the hot and wet spot between them. Dinner, all but forgotten, he grabbed her chin and turned her face toward his. When he captured her lips, his fingers sank into her, and her mouth opened to him. Her fingers were so tightly wrapped in his hair that he felt individual strands pull loose, but he didn't care.

Releasing her mouth, he returned to her ear. There was no need for him to whisper, as they were the only ones in the house, but she still seemed to need the reminder of that night. "You came all over my fingers, like you would gladly do now if I let you."

She tried to turn her head back to look at him, but he didn't move, holding them both in that position. His fingers continued working in and out of her while he squeezed her breast through the shirt.

"Do you have any idea how badly I wanted to bury myself in you that night?" he asked.

She shook her head.

"Especially after we heard someone coming. The idea of getting caught while inside you had me feral."

He was glad he hadn't followed that instinct once he saw the boys, but it didn't change the initial desire. He wanted to claim her, to make her his.

"I stopped myself that night, but now..." he trailed off, and his hand gripped the front of his shirt again and pulled, popping every button. She gasped and moaned at the same time. He pulled his fingers from her and slid his pants down. She was like putty in his hands, allowing him to move her however he wanted, and right now, he wanted inside of her. Bending her over the barstool, he spread her legs, lined up the tip of his cock, and slid into her pussy. She was so ready for him that he didn't even have to work his way to reach bottom. "You stay so fucking wet for me."

"Yes, fuck. I need it."

"You're so greedy. That kid would have never been enough for you. You need a man who can read your body and give you what you need."

He reached up and grabbed a handful of her hair, turning her, so he could see her face. She looked at him with hooded eyes, and when she opened her mouth to say something, he pounded into her harder and faster until all that left her mouth was moans. She leaned up on her arms and started pushing back into him.

"Not this time, little minx." Grabbing her elbows, he pulled her arms back until he could hold her back bowed. Never missing a stroke or slowing down, he fucked her long and hard until she went silent, every muscle in her body tightening. "Mmmmm that's it, Pretty, soak my cock." When he felt her orgasm subsiding, he slowed his strokes and let her arms flop forward. Her chest lay against the stool, as she tried to catch her breath. "You feel so good wrapped around my cock, still squeezing me like you want more. Are you still greedy for it?"

"Yes," she said, her voice hoarse.

Sliding into her fully, he leaned over her draped body. "Food first," he said next to her ear and withdrew from her completely. She made a slight whining sound and turned a hard glare on him. He simply smiled and, after washing his hands, opened the takeout containers.

CHAPTER 20

SHAR

S he tried holding onto her irritation, but the smell of the food forced her to focus on a different need. They hadn't eaten all day. Hell, she'd barely drunk any water, which likely explained why her voice was so hoarse. And after her drinking spree last night, it was surprising her pussy could still get wet. At that thought, she snuck a sideways glance at the man next to her. Not only could she not believe she was in his house, but she also could not believe how well he'd taken care of her in all ways.

"I don't know if I ever said it or not but thank you."

He smirked before answering. "For what?"

She pursed her lips and drew her brows together before releasing the tension in her face. "For last night. You didn't have to step in or take care of me, but you did, so thank you."

"Why did you do it?" he asked, never taking his eyes off her.

That was a great question. Why did she do it? Would it make sense to tell him that she was aggravated? Would it be enough to say it was his fault? Was that the truth?

"A moment of spitefulness and insecurity maybe," she said with a shrug trying to play off the uncertainty.

"Insecurity?" His face scrunched up in confusion. "You are probably the most secure woman I've ever met."

She smiled at that. If he only knew. "i have my moments."

"Seriously, though. Without sounding smug or egotistical, not that I can't be," he said with a wink, and she looked away to keep from laughing. "I can't help but feel like you made that choice in response to me stopping by yesterday afternoon."

It took a few moments before she could bring herself to look back at him. She didn't want to be having this conversation. She didn't want to admit that he made her feel things she'd never felt before.

"If I'm being honest, maybe a little, but probably not for the reason you think. It's not important, though. I simply wanted to thank you for showing up when you did."

He snorted a laugh, and her brows drew together. "You mean, you want to thank me for stalking you all night." Her mouth opened and then closed. He laughed again. "Look, I don't know what in the hell this is between us, but there's something about you that has my thoughts all over the place."

She took another bite of her food. She had to play off the fact that he was saying exactly what she was feeling. She wasn't ready to admit any of this.

"I wanted to invite you to dinner that night in Cali, but you were gone when I got back to the hotel. I wanted to invite you out last night, but you were already leaving with that young dude before I could get back from taking a shower. You moved too damn quickly on me both times."

"Oh, so you being slow is my fault now?" She brought her hand up to her face to hide her smile.

"Don't pretend you're offended. You're used to moving on, I'm guessing."

She looked at her plate of food and used her fork to stir things around without actually seeing any of it. "Is it really moving on if there was nothing there in the first place?"

He didn't say anything in response, just turned back to his

meal. She thought he might argue that there was something between them, and she was glad he didn't. At the same time, she knew there was something. This was all so unnerving. They sat in silence, both pretending to eat for what felt like hours. He'd pick up his fork, stab at something on the plate, and then put the fork down again. Occasionally, he'd glance her way and look like he wanted to say something but change his mind and repeat the pattern.

"This is very weird. Maybe it's time I go back to the hotel."

He looked at her, and there was something in his gaze this time that grabbed ahold of her insides. Something powerful and unsaid.

"This is new for me too. I've not had a woman in my house, as a guest, in a long time, and I don't want you to go." He reached out and grabbed her hand. "We don't have to talk any more. How about we watch a movie?"

She gave him a soft smile. "My choice?"

"Of course." He returned her smile and pulled her from the stool.

When she slid across the stool, her body reminded her of the pounding she had taken. Suddenly, she was aroused all over again and hoping he meant for them to go back to the bedroom for the movie. He didn't. Instead, he led her in the opposite direction, down a hallway she hadn't paid any attention to. At the end of the hall was a stairwell that led downstairs. They made their way down to a wide-open space that was fully furnished. This space was meant for entertaining. There was a pool table, a ping-pong table, and a full bar.

"Do you entertain often?"

"No, not as often as I'd like, honestly. I'm usually too busy or traveling."

"I feel you on that. Seems like a wasted opportunity for this space to not be used. It's lovely."

"Thank you."

He pulled on her hand, and they ventured past the game area to a dark hallway. He flipped on a light, and she saw a dark curtain drawn along the far end of one of the walls. He grabbed a set of remotes and led her behind the curtain. There were numerous types of seats on different platform layers, then a fan kicked on above their heads and lights came up on the far wall. The projection screen lit up with various streaming options.

"Wow!"

She had no other words for what she was seeing. She'd never known anyone to have a full theater in their house. Everything she saw here was a far cry from her first impression of him on his surfboard. Even after she'd realized he was older, and he had rocked her world that first night, she wouldn't have imagined this was where he lived.

"Yeah. I love this room. It's probably the one space, other than my bedroom, where I spend the most time. At least when I get a chance."

"You surprise me, Mack. Just when I think I have you figured out, you surprise me."

He walked her up to the second tier and climbed onto one of the mattresses with lots of pillows. He propped himself up, so he was half seated, and he gestured for her to join him. She climbed over the pillows until she could sit next to him. He put his arm around her back, so he could grip her waist. Once she was settled, he showed her how the system worked and handed her the remote.

"If you already know what you want to see, whether it is old or still currently showing in theaters, you can also talk into the remote by pressing that microphone button."

"Seriously? I feel like I stepped into a sci-fi movie here with all of the gadgets and gizmos."

He laughed. "This is nothing. The system in my office, though not quite as large, puts all of this to shame."

She looked at him, eyes wide. He simply shook his head

and pointed toward the screen. She wanted to ask about his job, but she didn't want any more weird and uncomfortable conversations tonight. Maybe she'd get a chance tomorrow. She scrolled through the television channels and didn't find anything interesting, so she opted for a romcom that had released recently. The only thing they were missing was the movie theater popcorn.

"Have you seen this movie before?"

"No, but I read the book it's based on, and I really liked it."

He watched her as the opening credits rolled. She tried not to let his stare unnerve her.

"You've Got Bookmail?" The fact he had read the title as a question made her laugh.

"How'd you see that when you've been staring at me the whole time?"

"I have good peripheral vision, but there's nothing on that screen that will outshine you."

She leaned into him, pushing his shoulder with her own. "My, aren't you the flirt tonight?"

"Is it working?"

"Maybe," she said and turned her attention back to the screen. She snuggled closer to him and settled in to watch the movie.

When it got to the ferris wheel scene, he blurted, "That's so unrealistic. Lots of people would be able to see them each time they went around."

She laughed. "This coming from the man who went 'feral,'" she said, making air quotes around the last word, "when he thought we'd get caught with his fingers inside me."

He grunted, which made her laugh harder. She looked up at him, and his stare had her nipples hardening. Fuck, he was sexy as hell. She was still wearing the button down he'd popped all the buttons from, and all she wanted was to feel his skin against hers. She turned onto her side, facing him, and ran her hand up under his t-shirt. When she found his left nipple and dragged her nails across it, he hissed. She repeated the action with his right nipple, and he moaned. This encouraged her to keep going. She pulled his shirt up and worked her way up his body until she was kissing her chest. She used her tongue and flicked his hardened nipples. His breath caught and heat pooled between her legs.

Turned on, she slid herself down his body and licked right above his waistband. His dick was already hard, and when she pulled the band down slightly, the tip was standing at attention right in front of her. She licked the drops of precum that had escaped the tip and then popped the head completely into her mouth. he moaned appreciatively, and she hummed around the head.

"Damn, woman, that shit feels so good."

She laughed and pulled his pants the rest of the way down, leaving her open access to his fully erect cock. she slid her fingers up the length of his shaft and then followed them with her tongue. His eyes watched her every move, and when she looked toward his face, his eyes were hooded. She took him in her mouth fully, continuing to hum along the head and shaft, even after he was against her throat. He grabbed her hair and held her down when she hit bottom. She moaned, and his hips bucked up. When he released her, she slid her mouth off of him. Saliva streamed from her mouth. Then she lifted the shaft and worked her tongue around his sack. His breaths started coming faster now, and when she took his balls into her mouth, he growled deep in his throat.

"You like that, do you?" she asked, her voice husky in arousal.

"Yes, and I want more."

"oh really, greedy, old man?"

She laughed at the look on his face and then took his cock back into her mouth, working it up and down in time to her hand working his shaft in an opposite direction. His legs stiffened, as her movements sped up. She wanted to make him lose control just once. It was one thing for him to lose his composure when he'd come, but it was another for her to have taken control and made him lose his shit.

Getting up on her knees, she gave herself a better position to access all of his cock and take the entire thing down her throat. He put his hand on the top of her head and tried to maneuver her at his pace. She wasn't stopping, slowing, or letting him gain the upper hand. Then he ran his other hand over her ass, sliding his fingers along her slit. He wasn't playing fair at all. His thumb found her clit and started making small circles, pressing harder and harder until she was panting around his dick. When she moaned and her legs shuddered, he slid two fingers inside of her, and her mouth opened wide, letting him slide out.

"That's not fair," she said. Her breaths were erratic, and she stuttered out the words.

"Is it not? How about this then?" He reached around her hips with his other hand and hauled them over his face, quickly slipping his tongue between her lips to find her swollen clit. She shuddered again and then grabbed his cock in her hand. She would not let him win this contest. She started working him with long strokes of her hand, lapping her tongue around the tip and sucking on it before sliding it back into her mouth. It was becoming harder and harder to hold her shit together when he was fingering her so well and flicking her sensitive clit with his tongue. He wrung a strong moan from her lips, and then she tightened them around his cock, sucking for all she was worth.

He moaned against her clit, and that was all the encouragement she needed. She maintained her steady pace of tongue, lips, and fingers along his shaft until his toes curled in.

"Shit, yes, suck that dick. Fuck, you do that so fucking well."

While he was distracted from her clit, she used her other hand to massage his balls. It wasn't long before they tightened in her grip and his cock swelled in her mouth. His fingers pulsed in and out of her until she couldn't hold back any longer. No sooner had he found his release in her mouth than she was moaning her own. Her legs were shaking, and after licking up every drop of his cum, she collapsed on top of him. He idly massaged her ass cheeks that remained in his face until she was able to move.

"You were a determined little minx, weren't you?"

"I don't know what you mean, sir."

A low grumble escaped his throat when he laughed at her response. When she finally felt capable of moving, she rolled off him, but didn't bother to turn herself around. She left her feet up by his head and lay her head on his thigh to finish watching the movie.

CHAPTER 21

SHAR

The following day, they stopped by her hotel for a change of clothes. They spent the day walking along the beach and enjoying each other's company. There was a quiet calm that had settled between them. The sexual tension had leveled off into a calm desire that came to a head multiple times throughout the day, but things were slow and sensual.

"What do you have on your agenda for tomorrow?" he asked. She heard the apprehension in his voice.

"I have a meeting in the morning and something a little later before I head to the airport."

"You're leaving tomorrow then?"

She sighed and gave him a small smile. She wasn't ready to leave him, but her time was up. "Yes. What about you?"

"I, too, have a meeting in the morning. It's like work never ends. As you know, I was traveling half of last week, so I'm still catching up."

"That makes sense."

Seated on the patio, looking out over the bay, they both fell silent. She ran her hand over his, and he linked his fingers with hers. Shar didn't know what to say. She wasn't even sure what she'd want to say if she could find the words. All these thoughts and feelings were so new for her that she wasn't sure what to do with them. Finally, he spoke.

"So where is home for you?"

"Are you meaning now, or like my hometown where I grew up?"

"Both, either. Whatever you want to tell me."

She let out a little laugh. "I'm from a poor town in Arkansas. We called it the city because we didn't know any better, but it was definitely not a city."

"I feel that. I am also from a small town but in the Midwest."

"Really? I don't hear any type of accent."

"I've tried really hard to get rid of it."

She chuckled. "I've tried really hard to hide it. When I'm stressed, it comes out more."

He pulls her hand up to kiss it. "So where is home now?"

"I live in Housington. I prefer the ocean, but I make do with our giant lake."

"Oh wow. So, you travel all over for work?"

She smiled up at him. "Yeah, my agent is my best friend, so he knows how to pimp me out, so to speak."

He chuckled. "So, he's your pimp?"

"Well, for work. I'm usually pretty good at getting my own dick."

"I can see that."

She turned herself around until she could straddle his lap. "Oh, can you now?"

His hands reach around, grabbing her ass, and pulling her against his groin. "Yeah, I can definitely see you having no problem getting dick when you need it."

Grinding herself against him, she made small circles, feeling his erection grow beneath her. It was a heady feeling.

"You can have this dick whenever you want it," he said, his voice deep and raspy.

She was still surprised that he'd been able to keep up with her all this time. She'd never met a man who could handle her, especially not an older man. Even when he'd been tired, he'd managed to ensure she was satisfied in all the ways that counted. Not to mention that he'd been great company these past couple of days and easy to talk to. Even the hard conversations were made easier by the sense that he legitimately wanted to get to know her. Likewise, she had been happily taking him in, learning what he enjoyed and where he was from. They both had shaky childhoods, but somehow, they both not only survived but thrived. They hadn't gotten into specifics about their current lives other than to realize that a regular weekend rendezvous would be difficult because of schedules and the distance. She didn't push for more information because she didn't want to ruin the time they were having by hoping for the impossible. She would just enjoy the time they had together and then go on with her life like she always did.

She reached between them and pulled his hard cock from his shorts. Once again, she was wearing little more than one of his shirts. As she slid down on him, letting him stretch every inch of her, she begged time to slow down.

Early the next morning, Mack brought Shar to her hotel to prepare for her business meeting and photo shoot. Of course, she didn't tell him all of that. She simply said that she had some things to do for work. He also claimed to have business to take care of when she saw how sexy he looked in his impeccably tailored blue suit. As soon as he dropped her at the hotel entrance, she missed his presence. She didn't have time to dwell on those feelings, though, as her ride would be there shortly to retrieve her.

Without a moment to spare, she was showered, dressed, and in the hired car on her way to the tech giant's headquarters. It was off the island, but Shar didn't care. The company was paying for the car and driver, so she took full advantage of the ocean-view hotel Jerry had negotiated for her. She certainly got more than she bargained for this week with that view.

Mack's beautiful face came to her mind as she thought about the dinner they shared last night. She would never think to claim it was a date, but the way he looked at her certainly made her feel like it was more than just two strangers fucking. She shook her head, trying to clear the thought from her mind. It would do her no good to begin imagining something more from what was meant to be a beach fling. She would be going home tomorrow, and today was filled with meetings and a very lucrative photo shoot. If all went well, she would need to give Jerry a huge bonus.

Shar was ushered into the boardroom on the top floor of the high-rise office building. There were already others seated around the table, including Jerry and her favorite photographer, Jacques. Henri was there too with who she presumed was his agent. Her chest tightened when Henri looked her way with a grin. She had completely forgotten the uncomfortable situation from last week thanks to Mack's distraction. Jerry stood with a smile and gestured to the seat he had saved for her between himself and Jacques who was also smiling in her direction.

"Good morning, gentlemen," she said in greeting.

Before she could get comfortably settled, the company owner's administrative assistant, Janet, came to the door to let them know Mr. Sloan Mackenzie was on an important phone call and would be here as soon as he finished. Shar hated being made to wait for a meeting like this. The delay was disrespectful to the people in the room. Hopefully, this wasn't a bad omen for how the rest of the day would go.

Her phone vibrated, and since the meeting hadn't begun, she opened the screen. It was a text from Mack.

> Mack--Hey, I just wanted to make sure you made it to whatever you needed to do for work.

> I did, thank you.

> Mack--I know you're leaving tomorrow. Can I see you tonight?

> That would be nice.

She pressed the send button and immediately heard a phone beep right outside the door that was already opening. Thankfully, everyone's attention was drawn to the sound, so no one registered her inaudible gasp as Mack walked through the door looking down at his phone.

"I'm so sorry I'm late. There was something that needed my direct attention."

He walked to the front of the room still not looking up at anyone. A small smile played at the edge of his lips. When he finally put his phone down on the table and looked around, that smile fell, and his eyes widened as they locked on Shar. Her pulse quickened and bile rose in her throat. She didn't play where she worked, and the realization that she had just spent the last two days fucking the man who would be signing her paychecks made her wish she hadn't had breakfast. She watched as determination replaced the shock in his eyes.

Mack began going over plans for the new ad campaign that Shar would star in. Across the table from her, Henri sat stoically. If she had been able to compile a coherent thought, she might have wondered what he was thinking, but she was unable to give him any head space. According to the plan, the two of them would be placed in various scenarios for short video recordings and photo opportunities as a way of demonstrating the potential of the company's new cell phones. In addition to the already contracted salary, each of them would receive a phone with lifetime upgrades.

Shar was only half listening. Though the initial nausea had subsided, her heartbeat still blasted in her ears. All she could think was that Mack had hired her for this job and then seduced her for the entire week prior. Had this been his intention all along? Did she not get the job on the merit of her previous work? She glanced at Kevin Dulaney, the Marketing Director for Velocity. He had said she was chosen because she was able to give the impression of being every woman. She thought that had meant she was versatile, not that she was easy.

"Excuse me," she blurted and made her way down the hall to find a ladies room.

Thankfully, there was no one else in the restroom, but she closed herself in the stall just in case. She needed a moment to pull herself together. Did it matter why she was hired? Not really. The contract was still valid. What did matter was the time they had spent together, especially the last two days. It was the first time in forever that she had started to feel a connection with someone beyond sex. If this was all a ploy by him, what did that mean for that connection and her ability to read people?

That was the part she was struggling with. She would, of course, do the job she had been paid for, but what would this week have cost her? Shar took a few more steadying breaths, left the stall, and splashed water on her face. She was still Sharlene Maxwell, and she could take on anything, including her own heart.

The ladies room was down the hall and around the corner from the boardroom. The rest of the floor was practically empty, unlike most tech companies she'd seen before where there were cubicles in every corner. Up here, there were just hallways and lines of doors that led to what she could only presume were offices. She made her way in the direction she had come when a strong hand grabbed her arm and pulled her through one of the doors.

"What the?"

She took a deep breath, ready to scream, but the person twirled her around until her back was to their chest and put their hand over her mouth.

"Don't scream, Pretty. It's just me."

Her breath was ragged, partially from the surprise and partially from the awareness that she was held tight against him. She forced herself to relax, though, so he would let her mouth go.

"Mack, what's all this about?"

She hadn't planned to ask him. Honestly, she was never going to speak to him again once they left that boardroom. Now that they were alone in an office, however, she couldn't let it be.

"What do you mean," he asked against her ear before trailing his lips down her neck.

"Stop it," she screeched, spinning out of his arms. "Did you plan this when you hired me?"

"What the fuck are you talking about?"

"This week, seducing me, not telling me that you're my fucking boss!"

"You think I knew that?"

"Didn't you? It's your signature on my fucking contract. My headshot was included in the packet my agent sent."

He released her completely, but she couldn't read his expression. "You're right. I should've known."

Tears stung the backs of her eyes, but she refused to cry. She would not feel sad about any of it. She would not feel guilty about any of it. She did not know who he was, so the guilt was not hers to bear. She turned to leave the room but stopped.

"I will fulfill the terms of my contract, but I just want you to know, I don't fuck where I work."

With that, she snatched the door open and walked back to the boardroom to retake her seat. Jerry had a concerned look on his face. She reassured him that she was feeling much better. Kevin Dulaney was at the front of the room giving finalized details for this afternoon's shoot. Shar sat back in her chair willing time to move faster, so she could get shitfaced alone in her hotel room.

CHAPTER 22

MACK

Mack went back to his office rather than the boardroom. Once again, he could've kicked himself for fucking things up. There had been no use in arguing the fact that he didn't know she was their chosen spokesperson because, while he didn't know, he should have. How many fucking times had Kevin asked him to look at her packet, to check out her photos? Why had he so stubbornly refused? Probably because he didn't care. He wanted to be more hands off with this campaign and let Kevin handle it. Truth be told, he was starting to consider stepping away from everything.

And then he saw her sitting on a chaise on a random beach behind a random hotel in California like she had been placed there just for him. After that, he couldn't have given two shits about any other women. If Kevin hadn't already been so excited about the spokesperson he had found, Mack might have introduced him to Shar even if she hadn't had any modeling experience. Oh, the irony of his bullshit. Fuck!

He opened the cabinet hidden between the bookshelves along the wall and poured himself a bourbon neat. He could walk back down to the boardroom and carry her out. He could bring her in here and hold her until she talked to him. "Dammit!"

"Whoa, boss, it's not even lunchtime."

"It's five somewhere, right?" Mack raised his glass in mock salute to Kevin.

Kevin walked into the office and closed the large oak door. He leaned back on it and crossed his arms. Mack took a deep breath, knowing that stance meant Kevin was willing to wait him out.

"You should have forced me to look at the models' packets."

Kevin raised a brow but still said nothing. Mack chuckled. What in the hell kind of life had he led to deserve this shit? He was generally good to people. Even when he had to let them down, he did it gently, trying not to hurt anyone's feelings. When he was with someone, they got his full attention, even when their time together was temporary. Shar was meant to be temporary. She intrigued him, but she wasn't supposed to be anything more than a blip on his time out there.

Looking out the window at the bay, Mack said, "She walked out of my dreams, and I was too damn stupid to recognize the coincidences."

"How many of those have you had already?" Kevin asked.

"This is my first, so not nearly enough." He lifted the half-empty glass again.

"Then, can you please stop talking in riddles, so I can try and help?"

"You can't help. What's done is done. It was great. No, better than great, but it's done now."

"Dude, what the fuck are you rambling about?"

"Shar! She's the woman from California." He turned back toward Kevin with his arms outstretched. Why was this so hard for the man to understand?

"Who is Shar?" Kevin had stepped away from the door and made his way to the couch along the side of the office.

"Our spokeswoman. You know, the fucking gorgeous blonde who spent all morning in our boardroom."

"Sharlene Maxwell?" Though he had asked it as a question, the look on Kevin's face said that he was trying to piece together everything Mack had said. Mack just watched him and waited for realization to dawn. "Sharlene is the woman you told me about. The one who left without a word after a crazy night together?"

"Yes, and fuck me, we just spent the entire fucking weekend together."

"Hold up, you did what now?" Kevin stood and walked over to the liquor cabinet to pour himself a drink. He held out the bottle to top off Mack's glass. "Dude, what were you thinking?"

"I didn't know. She told me her name was Shar late Friday night. I told her mine was Mack. We never exchanged anything formal, and now she's pissed at me." Mack flopped down into the nearest chair.

"Let me guess," Kevin said, putting the bottle away and walking back to the couch, "she thinks you hired her under false pretenses to get her here, or some other such shit." The man was way more intuitive than Mack.

Mack took another sip of his drink, letting the liquor warm him from the inside. He didn't know how he was going to make this right, but he knew he had to do something to fix this.

"I don't know what to do. I told her I didn't know, but she was right that I should have known. I should have known, and I should have stayed the fuck away from her."

"Why do you sound so dejected?" Mack looked up into Kevin's eyes at the question, and all Kevin could say was "oh" before taking a sip from his own cup.

They sat there in silence for what felt like an hour. Mack had no idea what was going through Kevin's head, but he was pretty sure he was trying to work out next steps for making sure this product launch went off without a hitch.

"If you're worried about having to find a new spokeswoman, don't," Mack said, shaking his head. "She said that she would still fulfill her contract before she stormed out on me. Oh wait, and before she spit out that she doesn't fuck where she works."

"Smart woman."

Mack glared at him.

"What? That is a smart rule to live by. Far less drama."

"You're supposed to be my friend right now." Mack leaned back in the chair and stared at the ceiling.

"I am your friend, and your business partner, and your marketing director. I can be all of those things at once and still be honest." Drawn by the sounds of Kevin moving around on the couch, Mack dropped his chin and found his friend looking straight at him. "Look, Mack, this is an awkward situation, but it is not the end of the world."

Mack groaned. "Kevin, if you tell me there are other fish in the sea or women in the bar, I'm going to call your wife and tell her to meet you at the ER."

Laughing, Kevin returned Mack's salute from earlier. "I wasn't going to say anything of the sort. I was going to remind you that contracts have end dates. She won't be working for or with us forever, just a year."

Mack closed his eyes, trying to tamp down his frustration at the whole situation and at Kevin's terrible attempts at empathy. When Kevin continued in his fix-it mode, Mack began shaking his head in exasperation.

"Hear me out. She will still be around often because of the work we've contracted her for. You will get to see her should you choose to see her, or you could just bide your time until the contract expires. If you still want her at that point, I will help get you together."

"What are you a fucking matchmaker?"

"Well, I did put you both in the same place at the same time."

"Shut the hell up." Mack said, standing up from the chair to walk around toward the wall of windows.

Would he be able to be in her vicinity for a year and keep his hands off of her? Would he be able to not push her to break her own rule? Hell, he had already broken his. He wasn't supposed to get involved, ever. Be their friend. Be their occasional lover. Never let them get too close. How the fuck did she get so close in such a short period of time.

"You know, she spent the weekend at my house," he said to Kevin without turning around.

"You invited her to your house? You never take women home."

"Not exactly an invite. I followed her to a few bars and stopped the young kid she was with from assaulting her. She was in shock and clung to me, so I put her in my car and took her home. I didn't know which room she was in at the hotel, and I didn't want to leave her alone. I didn't think. I was pissed off at her for putting herself in that position."

"Wait, you said you followed her. Why? That's a bit stalkerish."

"Because I had come back to the hotel to ask her out when I saw her leaving with that dude."

"So, she had a date already with someone else, and you followed them around?"

"No, ass, she did not have a date with someone else." His tone was mocking. I was just too stupid to tell her I was coming back for her. I got a little too full of myself and she went searching for someone else." After a pause, he finished. "Man, I feel guilty enough about all of this without you adding to it with your questions and judgments."

Kevin got up from the couch and puts his hand on Mack's shoulder. "You really like this woman?"

"Yeah, man. Something about her calls to me, makes me

feel settled and calm. I don't know what it is, but the entire world faded away this weekend when it was just she and I."

"And it's not just the sex then?"

"No," he said, shaking his head emphatically. "Don't get me wrong, the sex is amazing, but that's not it."

"Ok, then we will play this out. I will keep an eye on her, make sure she's here as often as possible. You will do your best to let her breathe and just be a silent partner in the marketing components, except for those planned trips and conferences that we can't pull out of. When the contract is finished next year, you'll ask her out like a normal fucking person, not a stalker."

Mack laughed. It was a dry laugh. There was no real mirth behind it. A whole year? Could he stay away from her for a whole year knowing how close she was regularly? He took another deep breath, looked up at Kevin and nodded.

"Thanks, man. I appreciate you."

"You better! Now, I have other shit to do today besides getting drunk with your ass."

Kevin tapped his glass to Mack's, downed the last of his drink, and sat it on the table.

Mack stayed where he was for a long time. He wasn't quite sure how much time had passed until Janet came to the door and asked if he wanted anything for lunch. He didn't respond at first, but when she told him she was going down for a fish sandwich, he looked up. He couldn't do anything about Shar right now, but he damn sure could go see what was up with Janet and Charlie.

"I'll come with you," he said. "I need to get some air anyway."

"Yes, you do! This room smells like a frat house."

His lips quirked up. He knew she couldn't smell the liquor, but the glasses were obvious, and he hadn't closed the cabinet door back yet.

"I'll clean it up, Momma J."

CHAPTER 23

SHAR

Shar flung herself on the bed as soon as she walked into the room. What a shit show this day had become! She could not believe that Mack was Sloan Mackenzie. She also could not believe that she had no idea. He didn't tell her. Jerry gave her no indication. How in the hell did fate or coincidence put them in the same place across the country at the same time only to bring them here and then break her heart. Wait, was her heart breaking? Is that what this ache was? How? She'd never let anyone in before. She didn't understand what was happening between her and Mack, but she damn sure didn't think it was anything that might already cause her heartache. No. She was just pissed because she would now have to give up the best sex she'd ever had with the sexiest man she'd ever met because he just had to be her fucking boss. Hell, she had said no to Henri, and he was only going to be her co-star in these campaigns. There was no way she could continue seeing Mack when it went against her major rule.

She sat up and grabbed a pillow. With a screech of frustration, she threw it across the room. Feeling better for that little bit of aggression, she grabbed another and repeated the action. Soon, all the pillows were off the bed. She was looking for other items she could throw when someone knocked on the door.

"What?" she yelled, not wanting to be bothered with anyone.

"Are you okay in there?" Jerry's voice came back through the doorway.

"Go away, Jer. I don't have it in me to chat."

"All the more reason for you to let me in. You need me."

She fought hard not to smile at his egotism. She did need him. She needed her best friend, but how could she explain what she was going through and that it was all because of the best weekend she'd had in probably ever.

"Hold on." She ran around the room tossing the pillows back onto the bed. He could see it's a disheveled mess, that she was a disheveled mess, but he didn't need to see the full extent of it.

As soon as she opened the door, Jerry waltzed in. He was empty-handed, which meant he wasn't there to talk about work. She eyed him skeptically.

"What's up?" she asked, with as much enthusiasm as she could muster, which was none.

"That's my question, Sharlene."

Jerry almost never used her full name, unless she'd stepped over some boundary or acted a fool. She didn't recall doing either today, but most of the morning was a blur. She hadn't listened to half of what had been said, and she barely registered the packet of information that was haphazardly tossed onto the desk across the room. All she could picture was Mack walking into the boardroom, a smile on his face, looking down at his phone, at her text, and she ached all over because of it. She crawled back on the bed and curled into a ball. Jerry climbed up behind her and curled himself around her.

"I have all day. If this is what you need, I got you."

Shar opened her mouth to say something, and her throat closed with emotion. She was always grateful for Jerry and their friendship, but this was different. She hadn't needed to be held like this since the day she learned her mother had died. She had gotten the call that her mother was found in a seedy hotel room covered in her own vomit, multiple condoms in the trash, all with different DNA, and the hotel records showed she'd checked in nearly a week prior. Sharlene, because she was little Sharlene in that moment, had so many emotions she couldn't work through. She called Jerry, and within minutes, he was at her house, holding her, rocking her, and just being there. He was more than she deserved.

"Thank you," she finally squeaked out before a sob threatened to take over.

He held her for what felt like hours. When she finally felt like it was time to move, she sat up.

"I need a drink."

"Do you want to go out and maybe get some dinner, or do you want me to run out and bring some stuff back?"

She thought about that question for far longer than it warranted. Did she want to go out? Yes, actually. She wanted to get out of this room and out of her head. She wanted to pretend that things were normal, and she'd just had a fun little fling that was over before she traveled back home. That wasn't the reality, though. She was safe here in the room. This island was Mack's home. He owned a house here. He could literally be anywhere they might go. She wasn't sure how she'd respond to seeing him again today. This morning, she'd managed to hold onto her anger because the shock was so fresh. She wasn't angry anymore, and she damn sure didn't want to start crying in front of him out in public.

"It's probably a better idea if you bring something back."

Jerry nodded, grabbed his jacket and a key card from where she'd thrown it on the dresser, and he was gone. She wasn't worried about what he'd bring. They'd been friends so long that he probably knew her likes and dislikes better than she did at this point. Taking advantage of the empty room, she stripped out of her clothes and stepped into the shower. She stood under the cold stream unflinching while it warmed. When she had scrubbed away all she could, none of it touching the painful itch to reach out to Mack inside, she walked back into the room and found some lounge pants and a t-shirt. She would not be leaving the room, so she threw her wet hair up in a messy bun and sat on the balcony listening to the surf while she waited for Jerry to return.

She took the time to scroll through her phone. She had never been big on social media. With the childhood she'd had, she never wanted to reconnect with people she'd known back then. That's why she'd started introducing herself by the shortened version of her name and changed her age as well. She probably should have just changed her name completely, but she couldn't bring herself to do that after her mother was gone. It was the only thing she had left from the woman, and part of her needed to believe that her mother had loved her back then. Her eyes started burning at the thought of her mother and how often she'd felt unloved due to the decisions Carolyn Maxwell made. It was hard to forgive the pain, neglect, fear, and near assaults she'd endured all those years. Not to mention the embarrassment and insecurity every time she'd enter a new school or disappear for months before returning to school.

Think about something else, Sharlene. Yes, how about learning more about the company she'd be working for this next year. Clicking into her browser, she typed in Velocity Communications Inc. Right at the top of their website was a picture of Mack, and her breath caught. All she'd have had to do was a quick search for the company's website, and she'd have known her surfer was also about to be her boss. What a mind fuck. Maybe she just really didn't want to know. Maybe that was the problem. Maybe she was the problem. He was as easily found as she was, and yet she never thought to look. Hell, when they talked about their childhoods, they never even broached the subject of who they were today aside from the time they spent together. Was he just as hands off in terms of relationships as she was? Did he never wonder what would happen when she left and whether he'd wanted her to leave any less than she wanted to leave? Were her feelings all one-sided.

Her phone chimed with a text message. Thinking it was Jerry saying he was on his way back, she clicked over to the messaging app.

Mack--I know you don't want to talk to me, and I don't expect an answer. I simply want to say I'm sorry. You're right. I should have known. I'm glad you have still agreed to work for the company because I think you are the best person for the job, and I will leave you to do that job. I had a great weekend, and I don't regret not one minute beyond not responding fast enough Friday night.

She dropped the phone in her lap, tears streaming down her cheeks. She sniffed and tried to rub them away, but they just kept coming. He didn't regret their weekend. He regretted the fact that they didn't know who each other was. What exactly did that mean? Would he have stayed away had he known? Did he have the same rule? Did he have any rules? All the talking they did about their lives, not once did they bother to talk about the things that mattered. What in the hell, Mack?

She laughed at herself, at the tears coupled with her blaming him. This wasn't any more his fault than hers. They both could have known. The question was, what did she want now that she did know? How could she move on with these feelings that were brewing for him. Fuck, this whole situation was fucked.

Just then, Jerry came through the door hauling bags and drinks. He'd found some frozen margaritas and stopped at the bar for two glasses of wine.

"Did you know that they don't sell liquor in the grocery

stores or gas stations here? They have a special store for that. I didn't want to drive to the other end of the island for it, so I grabbed what I could get and then ordered some wine downstairs. If we need more, I'll have them delivered to the room."

After setting everything down, he looked at her and saw the tear streaks on her face.

"What happened? You weren't fine when I left, but you damn sure weren't crying."

He opened his arms, and she walked into them with a sob. She handed him her phone that was still open on the text message, and he gasped upon reading it.

"Um, is this Mack Sloan Mackenzie?" Shar nodded, rubbing her tears into his shirt. "Do you want to tell me what this text is in reference to? Did you see him after the meeting and threaten to quit?"

Shar looked up into his eyes, which were huge with concern, though this time for the contract he had negotiated. She forgot he didn't have all the details when she had handed him the phone.

"Let's eat, and I'll try to make it make sense. No promises." With that, she grabbed the bag of food and carried it over to the small island that served as a table in the suite.

Jerry grabbed the drinks and followed her. Shar immediately grabbed one of the frozen margarita pouches and popped the straw in like a juice box. She brought the straw to her lips intending to only take a small sip, but she sucked down nearly half of the drink. Immediately, she pressed her palm against her forehead, and Jerry bust out laughing.

"Rude," she said, her eyes squinting as she tried to wait for the pain to release. He laughed even harder, and she slapped at him but missed. Then she started laughing. It felt so much better to laugh, even at her own expense, than to cry.

"So, tell me what this is all about."

Jerry started pulling the food containers out of the bag.

There was some takeout Chinese, which was her favorite comfort food. She smiled at him and took a quick bite of the rice with a satisfied sigh before starting the story.

"Do you remember that guy I told you I met in California? The one who I saw again here last week."

"The one you let fondle you in public?"

She narrowed her eyes at him but then nodded. "Yes. I spent the entire weekend with him."

"Really? That's a good thing, right?"

"No," she said, her voice cracking. "I spent the weekend with my boss, not knowing he was my boss. Now I don't know what to do." Tears welled in her eyes again, and she tried to brush them away.

Jerry put his hand on her shoulder. "Hey, this is so unlike you. What are you struggling with exactly?"

"You know my rule, Jer. I don't fuck where I work. I don't fuck around with people I work with, let alone with someone I work for. I even told Henri no just last week because I found out we'll be working together, and I didn't really feel anything for him."

"So, the problem is that you have feelings for this Mack."

"No. Yes. No." She took a bite of food in her mouth.

"Well, it seems like Mr. Sloan Mackenzie is having a hard time with this situation as well."

She sobbed around the food she was chewing. Maybe it should make her feel better to know he, too, was struggling, but it didn't. She didn't want him to be upset. She wanted to be able to walk away unscathed, and that wasn't happening.

"So, what do you want to do about this, Shar?"

"Dammit, Jerry, I don't know." She took the phone back and looked at the texts again, trying to conjure her anger rather than the confusion and heartbreak she felt.

"What are you feeling for the man right now?"

Shar closed her eyes. "I like him. I genuinely like him. I'm pissed at him and myself about this situation, and I'm hating this rule that I have, which scares me."

Jerry was smiling at her when she finally opened her eyes. "So, let's work out a plan for how you can keep your job, finish your contract, and get your man."

She gave him a wan smile. She couldn't see any way of making all of that happen in her favor, but she was sure Jerry would come up with some kind of hair-brained plan.

CHAPTER 24

SHAR

The days after Shar arrived back home to Housington dragged. She had a hard time keeping her mind from Mack and all that had transpired on Wilmont Isle. As weeks passed, Shar told Jerry she was bored sitting at home every day. Though she had loved the idea of being able to take time off between publicity events and shoots because she was getting a monthly stipend, she never imagined how frustrating it would be to spend so much time alone with her thoughts. By the end of month two, Jerry was tired of her bitching.

"You need to get laid!" he yelled through the phone.

"Fuck you, Jer! I need to work. I can't do this sitting home for weeks at a time. I thought I'd have had more to do or more to occupy my time."

"Like I said, you've never gone so long without some dick. Yes, getting your rocks off always coincided with work, but it also calmed your ass down. Maybe just getting some without the work will have the same effect."

"You're being a real jerk, you know."

"No, I'm being your friend. How long has it been?"

"Since the day of that fucking board meeting."

"That was nearly two full months ago, Shar." His voice

had softened, and Shar thought maybe she could get him to see her side of the argument. Then he finished with, "How long had your last drought been?"

She clenched her teeth before replying. "I'm not in a drought. I just don't fuck at home."

"Not at home. Not at work. Not your boss."

"Don't be an asshole."

Jerry laughed on the other side of the connection, and Shar couldn't stop the corners of her mouth from pulling up too. "It's not funny," she said. "Get me a gig, please?"

"I can't," he said, his voice suddenly serious.

Before Shar could ask why, Jerry explained that he'd already gotten a call from Velocity. There was an upcoming conference in Italy that they wanted her at. She needed to pack and get ready to fly on Tuesday. There was no way to get her a gig, a flight, hotel, and return before she'd have to leave.

"Dammit, I was just there a couple weeks ago."

"You saw him again, didn't you?"

"No, and that was almost worse."

"Oh honey. You've got it bad. We talked about this. You would ignore him if he was there when you were working, and you would be grateful if he wasn't."

She flopped on the bed and lay back against the pillows. "I know, but that's so much easier said than done. I didn't seek him out though. I went on as if nothing was amiss."

"Good. And when you go on this trip, you're going to do whatever you need to stay away from him. Bring your favorite vibrator and get yourself off 4 times a day if you have to. Hell, it's Italy. Find you a Leonardo for the week."

She sat up straight. "We're going to be there for a whole fucking week? I don't know if I can be with him for that long and hold it together."

"That's why I'm telling you to get laid before you go or find someone there. Take the fucking edge off."

"You do know it's not just the sex I miss, right?"

"Yes, but I don't know what else to do to help, so work with me here."

Shar chuckled, and before she knew it, she was rolling in laughter on the bed. "Thanks, Jer. I do appreciate you. I'll start packing and remember to bring a friend with me."

"I love you, and I want you happy."

Shar was dressed casually as usual. She was already anxious about this trip, so there was no way she was going to wear something restricting. Thus, she had on a pair of black leggings with a crop top and a light jacket tied around her waist just because planes sometimes got cold. Her loose bun bobbled on the top of her head. As she made her way between the gate she'd just arrived at and the one she'd been directed to for their departure, someone called her name. Turning, she saw Kevin Dulaney, Velocity's marketing director, running in her direction.

"Sharlene, I'm so glad I caught you."

"What's up, Kevin?"

"Two things. They announced that our gate changed about 10 minutes ago, and we're all grabbing breakfast at the restaurant down on that end."

We? She knew Mack was the other part of that collective, and she wasn't ready to face him directly this early in the morning. "I'm not hungry. What's the new gate. I can just meet you all there."

Kevin eyed her for a few seconds before responding. "Are you sure?"

"Absolutely. I don't usually eat this early in the day. You two enjoy..."

"Three," he said.

Three? That was unexpected. Then she figured they might have invited Henri as well. She hadn't bothered to ask Jerry, even though Henri had not been at all the other shoots and events she'd attended the past couple months. "Sorry, you three enjoy your breakfast, and I'll see you at the gate."

As soon as he gave her the information, she turned on her heel and headed back in the direction she'd come. Though he, too, walked toward that direction, he didn't crowd her, and she didn't turn to watch where he turned off. With her head high, she made her way down the long hall toward the new gate number.

"Good morning, Sharlene," a woman's voice said, breaking through the audiobook Shar was enjoying. She looked up to see a beautiful woman, maybe mid-thirties, possibly early forties, with curly brown hair cropped into a cool pixie style. She held a white paper bag in her hand. Shar removed one of her ear buds.

"Good morning," she said warily. "Do I know you?"

"We've not met yet, but I've heard a lot about you. I'm Tabitha, Kevin's wife. The guys were still talking shop at the restaurant, so I offered to come sit with you rather than listen to them ramble on about presentations, WIFI speed, and device specs." She made an exasperated gesture and rolled her eyes.

Shar laughed. She liked this woman already. "Nice to meet you. When Kevin said there were three of you eating, I assumed it was the other model they hired with me."

"Nope, just me. When he told me they were going to Italy, I wasn't going to pass up the chance to see the country and get some authentic food like my nonna used to make."

"Lucky you to be able to enjoy the vacation. I don't even have the itinerary yet, so I'll likely spend the entire time stuck in a room of the conference center like the last conference we attended here."

"Oh, that would be a travesty. I'm sure I can talk Kevin

into letting me steal you away for some shopping or a lunch at least."

"That's sweet, and while it sounds far more interesting that playing game show hostess showing off devices, I know what I signed up for." Shar gave her a genuine smile.

"I'm so sorry," Tabitha said. "You were listening to something when I interrupted you. I'll let you get back to it. Oh, and here is something for later in case you get hungry." She handed Shar the paper bag.

"What is it?" Shar asked, perplexed.

"I don't know, actually. Mack ordered it and asked me to give it to you since I was coming this way sooner than them."

Shar eyed the bag with her brows knitted together. "That was nice of him, but I really am not hungry." Really what she wanted to say was that he could keep his damn peace offering if he couldn't bother to deliver it himself, but she wouldn't bring this stranger into the middle of their problems.

"That's fine. You don't have to eat it now, but you might get hungry on this flight and not want whatever it is they serve in first class."

Now, that was the truth. Usually, they served something that was barely edible, though sometimes she got lucky. She opened the bag and saw a bowl of some sort. She pulled it out of the bag and opened the lid. It was an egg scramble with bacon and cheese. She took a deep breath. That was the breakfast he had made her that Sunday morning she was at his house. Tears threatened to pool in her eyes. She quickly grabbed her water bottle and took a sip to stave them off.

"Do you read," Tabitha asked.

"Actually, I was listening to an audiobook when you came up."

"Oh really? What kind?" she asked in a conspiratorial whisper. "I'll show you my e-reader if you show me your audiobook collection."

Shar laughed aloud. Yep, she liked this woman. "You said

you're married to Kevin, right?" She laughed again, and Tabitha joined her in a giggle.

"Yep, for the past 5 years. We are complete opposites and perfect for each other."

"I was gonna say. He seems really stuffy, and you...well, you do not."

Tabitha laughed again and nodded. "He's a work in progress. He's always taken himself and everything around him way too seriously. He and Mack were two peas in a pod when I met them. Neither one of them able to take a moment and smell the roses. Their noses were both down at all times trying to get that business built to where it is now. Then Mack started surfing, and he finally found some kind of release that broke him from his all-work nature."

Shar just listened. It was fascinating to hear about the two men from someone else's perspective, someone who knew them both well. She smiled and nodded as Tabitha described them as workaholics and stubborn as fuck. She explained how she had to force her husband to take some nights off, and to turn off his laptop at home. She started buying tickets to the theater to make him shut down for at least one night a month, sometimes two if she was lucky.

"He likes to pretend he doesn't like our theater dates, but he's lying. He just didn't know what he was missing before he met me."

"Oh, I'm sure."

"I hope that one day Mack can find someone who makes him slow down and enjoy life too. He deserves it."

All Shar could do was smile. She didn't know if Tabitha knew anything about the history Shar and Mack shared. History, of course, was maybe pushing it a bit for the total of 4 nights they had spent together. One day she'd ask him, or her. To change the subject, she pulled out her phone and opened her audiobook app. When she passed it to Tabitha, the woman pulled out her e-reader and passed it over.

Shar scrolled. There was nearly every genre in here. Then she came to a book she knew and laughed aloud.

"Does Kevin know you read smut? He does not seem the type to be ok with such things," Shar says with a wink.

Tabitha laughed and shook her head. "He has no idea what I read. Often, I'm sitting right next to him reading about some poor woman getting DP'd in the back of a church, and he is oblivious, focused on his spreadsheets. He never turns me down when I want to try something new though, so it's all good."

"That's awesome! Once I finish the book I'm listening to, we can trade devices for the rest of the flight and/or the flight home. I think I have maybe 3 or 4 hours left."

"Sounds like a plan. Then you can listen to the two of them talk about work for the entirety of the trip. I'll just sit back and listen to sex."

Both women were red faced and laughing when the men walked up to them. They stood there watching for a few moments without saying a word, and Shar tried very hard to not acknowledge Mack's eyes on her. She felt his presence as soon as he walked into their waiting room, and it was hard to keep her heartbeat and breaths at a normal pace with his intense gaze burning into her skin.

"Looks like you two are getting along well enough," Kevin said, finally walking over and kissing his wife on the cheek.

"We share the same taste in books, and we talked about trading devices on the plane. I told her which of her books I'd like to listen to, so she could download it before we take off, and she did the same for my e-reader. We're now besties."

Shar took that moment to look at Mack, and he was still staring at her, his eyes scrunched together. His back was stiff, and his muscles taut, like he was holding himself still against his own will. She nodded in his direction as nonchalantly as she could muster. "Mr. Mackenzie. Good to see you again."

As soon as she said his name, time seemed to stand still.

His eyes opened wide. Tabitha turned to look at him, as if she hadn't realized he'd joined them as well, and Kevin's head swung back and forth between Mack and Shar like he was waiting for a fight to break out. There was no way she'd give anyone the satisfaction of a fight in public.

"Likewise," he finally managed to respond. "Kevin tells me that you've been doing a phenomenal job as our spokesperson. The print ads are showing everywhere, and the TV clips are getting traction. We've already had a number of preorders for the Version 2, and we hope that after these next couple of conferences, we'll have many more."

She could tell he was rambling. There was no reason she needed to know all of this. She was the face, not the brainchild, not an investor, and certainly not a business partner. "That's all wonderful. I'm glad things are working out so well."

"Speaking of the work Sharlene is doing for the company," Tabitha interjected, "I'm sure you can find a few hours where I could steal her away for some shopping or lunch or something, right?" She looked between Mack and her husband, her brows lifted high. She was clearly expecting an affirmative response.

Mack shrugged and lifted his chin toward Kevin. Kevin's eyes flitted all over the place before looking back at his wife. "We'll have to see what the conference looks like and how things are going." Tabitha's look never changed as she faced her husband. He swallowed, and Shar had to stifle a giggle at his discomfort. He obviously didn't like telling the woman no. "But I'm sure we can carve out some time for you two ladies to enjoy the trip." Tabitha smiled and patted his hand.

Shar shook her head and stuck the second earbud back in her ear, letting the narrator's voice drown out the uncomfortable wait. She could feel Mack's gaze on her repeatedly, but she successfully ignored him until he touched her elbow and tilted his head toward the gate. When she removed the earbud, he said, "They've called our flight." She gave him a light smile and grabbed her bag before following Kevin and Tabitha who were already having their tickets scanned.

Shar had never been in this type of plane before. There were only eight first class seats, and theirs had been turned to face each other. Apparently, Kevin had made the request of the flight attendants before Shar could make her way down the gangway. Tabitha was seated next to her husband across from Shar, which left the seat next to Shar empty for the man who already occupied too much space in her mind let alone at her side.

Mack walked into view and placed his carry-on into the overhead bin. His shirt lifted, giving her an open view of his abs, and her mouth watered. Fuck, why was this man so damn sexy? Why couldn't he be a toad or mean or something that would make him unattractive. When he took his seat, his shoulder brushed hers, and when he got comfortable, his leg brushed hers too. She had the urge to turn away from him but stopped herself. She didn't want to draw attention to her discomfort.

Tabitha pulled out her e-reader and settled her head and back against her husband's side. Mack scrolled through is phone, and Kevin pulled out his laptop as soon as the pilot allowed devices. Shar took all of that as her cue to turn her book back on and settle in. About an hour into the flight, she felt Mack's breath on her shoulder, and when she turned in his direction, she realized he was asleep. His head was leaned toward her without touching her, and his eyes were closed. She looked at their travel companions, but both were otherwise occupied, so she used the opportunity to really look at Mack.

Though his face was relaxed in sleep, he looked tired, like he had been going for weeks straight without a break. She wondered if he had even been out in the surf recently. She remembered the way his body moved on his board, and heat pooled in her core. She took in the length of his eyelashes and the shape of his lips. With a deep sigh, she sat up straighter, so his head could lean on her shoulder rather than just dangling in the air. A jolt ran through her body, but she held herself still to not wake him.

CHAPTER 25

MACK

Mack woke to a crick in his neck and the smell of gardenias filling his senses. He immediately knew that she was close, and he was afraid to look for fear she might disappear again. If he couldn't get close to her when he was awake, he would keep her in his dreams as long as possible. He listened carefully and heard nothing. Taking in a deep breath, he opened his eyes. Kevin was in the same position as when Mack fell asleep. The man never stopped working. Tabitha's shoulders and head were leaned on Kevin, but Mack couldn't tell if she was reading or sleeping. Slowly, he lifted his head slightly to look up at Shar. Thankfully, her head was turned away from him toward the window. He initially thought she was asleep, but then he caught her reflection in the window, and her eyes were wide open. He froze, waiting for her to see him looking at her and move away, but she didn't. She just looked out the window.

"Oh good, you're awake," Kevin blurted, startling everyone with his unnecessarily loud voice when they were all so close together.

Reluctantly, Mack lifted his head up from Shar's shoulder

and sat upright working his neck side to side trying to loosen it. "Yeah, did you need something?"

"Not exactly need, but I thought you might be interested in some of the calculations I've made."

Grabbing the flight attendant's attention to order a drink first, Mack then turned back to Kevin. "Okay, hit me with it."

"We had an amazing first quarter, far better than before."

"Of course, we did. We took a beating at the end of the year, and now we've put lots of new things in place, including our new spokesperson." He gestured toward Shar who turned to face them.

"No. I mean, this quarter has been better than any we've had in a long time."

Mack leaned forward, and Kevin swiveled the laptop, so he could see. When Shar leaned in over his shoulder, he looked up at her with a quick smile before turning back to the spreadsheet. "What is that number here?" he asked, pointing at the screen.

Kevin, focused on where Mack pointed and said, "that's the number of preorders we've had for Version 2."

"And this one?"

"That's the amount we've been offered by new investors."

"Whoa!"

Kevin nodded in agreement. "Whoa is right!"

"If we can close on some additional deals at the conference and get some more orders, we might have our best year yet."

Mack sat back against his seat and accepted the drink from the flight attendant. He took a sip and smiled. Glancing toward Shar, he noticed her brows drawn together.

"Is everything alright?" he asked quietly.

"What does all of that mean?"

"It means that you are helping Velocity have its best year financially since we first started. Thank you." He tipped his cup at her in a salute.

Tabitha sat up then and the women exchanged

pleasantries and devices. Tabitha put in a set of earbuds and leaned back in her seat. He noticed the open paper bag sitting against the wall between the women's chairs. The bowl was tipped precariously into the bag, meaning that Shar finally ate the scramble. She must have done so while he was sleeping. He smiled to himself and then chanced a look at her one more time. She had crossed one leg underneath her ass and the other crossed over top like she was doing a yoga pose, except she was leaned back with the e-reader in her hand. He looked over her shoulder at what she was reading, and his eyes grew large. He had seen and heard on social media that there were many books with sex scenes in them, but damn. He quickly took note of the book's title from the top of the page and typed it into his phone. He didn't want to get caught reading over her shoulder, but he wanted to see how that scene ended.

It was past dinnertime when they arrived at their hotel in Italy. Kevin complained of being tired and hungry. They all agreed to manage their own meals through room service for the night and to meet for breakfast the next morning. The concierge took Kevin and Tabitha up to their room first and promised to return for Mack and Shar's belongings. He must have assumed they were together since the other two were a couple. When they were alone, Mack asked Shar if she wanted to wait. He offered to help her up to her room if she didn't. He didn't mention that his room was right next door, not wanting to make her uncomfortable.

She shrugged before saying, "Either works. I just can't carry it all myself."

"I got you," he said, putting his own bag back over his

shoulder and grabbing her large suitcases to roll them toward the elevator.

At the room, she inserted the key, threw her purse and small bag in on the floor and turned back to drag the large suitcases inside. "Thanks for your help," she said. "Have a good night." And then she closed the door before he could say anything in return.

"Good night," he said aloud to the empty hallway before turning toward his own door.

After finishing his light dinner, Mack propped himself up against the headboard and focused on the book he'd watched Shar reading on the plane. It was wholly erotic. There was a bit of a story as well, but the story was built around sex. "Much like the weekend we spent together," he said aloud to himself. As his arousal grew, he found himself wishing he had a good reason to go knock on her door. It had been hard being so close to her without being able to close the distance. He had promised Kevin that he would refrain from initiating anything more than idle conversation with Shar until the contract was up. Every time he saw her, he regretted that promise.

What was the chance she was still reading the book on the other side of this wall? Would she hear a knock on it? Would she hear a scream and come running? He laughed and focused his attention back on the book. Just as he finished the chapter, a whimper came through the wall. *What was that?* He sat completely still and held his breath. He was about to settle himself back down into the bed when he heard it again, louder this time. *Was that her? Was she alright?* With a war waging between his head saying she would not appreciate him banging on her door in the middle of the night and his heart arguing that she might be hurt, he waited.

It took less time before the whimper came again, and again. It took another minute before his brain registered that what he thought were cries were actually moans. Hell, his dick had recognized them before he did because it was standing at attention. Fuck. He could only imagine what she was doing over there. He threw the blankets off himself ready to march over there when he heard her talking. *Was someone there with her?* Mack hadn't heard her door open and close. He hadn't even heard voices in the hall. No, he wouldn't even imagine her with anyone else. *But who was she taking to?*

Mack got on his knees and put his ear to the wall, at least as well as he could over the short headboard. Her moans were coming more frequently. *And what was that other sound? Was that? No, it couldn't be.* He leaned his forehead against the wall and let out a long exhale. He could picture her spread out on the bed, vibrator against her clit, writhing at the sensations. He didn't need to be in the room to imagine her working the shaft in and out of her tight pussy. Mack reached into his pajama bottoms and pulled out his cock. Between the sounds of her enjoyment and the visions of her passing through his mind, it was throbbing with need.

Now that he knew she was alone and what the other sound was, he flipped back over and put his back against the headboard again. He stroked his shaft from tip to root, squeezing at the bottom. As her moans grew louder, his strokes got faster and he squeezed tighter, imagining his cock slamming in and out of her. Then she said something again, but it was too muffled for him to make out.

"C'mon, baby, say it again for me." He had no idea what it was, but he'd give anything to have her talk to him while getting herself off.

His breaths were erratic, and his strokes still matched her moans. He was so close, and it was so hard to not come, but he was waiting for her. And then she screamed her release.

"Mack. Yes. Mack. I'm coming."

Hearing his name from her lips triggered his own release. He cried out as he came all over his hand and stomach. His body jerked, and his heart soared. She called his name. In her moment of release, she called for him.

His eyes kept sliding back over to her face throughout breakfast. He tried to play it cool and pretend like nothing happened last night, but what he really wanted to do was ask if she'd heard him come along with her. He wanted to provoke her like she had him. It didn't matter if she didn't know he was right on the other side of the wall. In fact, he didn't even want to think about someone else being over there listening to her moans of self-pleasure. He wanted to keep them all for himself. Thus, he kept his mouth shut.

"Is everything okay?" she asked, her brows knitted in concern.

He simply smiled and nodded, stuffing his mouth full of pancakes. She pursed her lips, clearly not believing him, and it only made his smile grow wider around the mouthful of food.

"What is the plan for the day?" Tabitha asked. "Does your conference actually start today?"

"There's registration and vendor set up," Kevin said in response. "There are also a couple of workshops, but we didn't sign up for any of them."

"Oh wonderful," she said clapping, "that means we can all go out and play tourists together."

Kevin groaned and Mack laughed. "Oh, c'mon, Kev. It could be fun. I've not been here before and neither have you. If your wife wants to drag you out sightseeing and shopping, and Shar here is amenable, why not?"

"Why not, indeed," Kevin said under his breath, squinting his eyes at Mack.

Though Mack smiled back, he could tell Kevin knew he was up to something. They had been friends too long. He wouldn't admit it if asked, but Mack wasn't about to turn away the opportunity to spend all day in Shar's presence.

CHAPTER 26

SHAR

After getting themselves registered for the conference, Shar and the two guys met Tabitha in the hotel lobby. The plan was to find a visitors' center and gather information for a walking tour they could take together. Along the way, they would grab lunch and maybe hit up one of the museums Tabitha had found through a quick Google search. Since no one else in the group had considered the possibility of having time to play tourist, they weren't much help in creating a plan. Shar was thrilled to be able to get outside of the hotel and see some of the beautiful city.

Tabitha and Kevin led the way arm-in-arm since she had the ideas, and he had the electronic map. Thankfully, Turin was one of the top tech cities, allowing them to have service to make their way around. The visitor center provided them with enough information and locations to keep them busy all week. They didn't have a week, so the group found somewhere to sit in the Piazza Castello and planned a more specific route.

"I do not want to walk around a park," Kevin complained. "We have plenty of parks back in the U.S."

"This is about experiencing the culture here, my dear. Just

bear with me and then we'll let you pick out where to have lunch." She patted Kevin's hand, which was on her leg.

Rather than affection, the move was placating, and Shar had to stifle a laugh. She felt Mack's gaze and turned her smile on him, playing off her mirth at the couple dynamics of their companions. Mack's eyes were soft and his smile genuine. She felt the pull to move closer to him, to melt against him, and she fought it. She raised a brow in question, and he shrugged.

"Is there anything specific you would like to see, Mr. Mackenzie?"

Some emotion passed across his face before he closed his eyes and took a deep breath. "Please call me Mack while we're out here. There's no need to be so formal on a tour."

"I could call you Sloan," she said, prodding him.

"I would prefer you didn't." There was a quiet demand in his tone, and her body responded in the most torturous way, her core tingling.

"Will you answer the question? What would you like to see?"

By this time, the other couple had worked through their disagreement and were watching the exchange she and Mack were having. She suddenly felt very uncomfortable under their scrutiny. Mack didn't seem bothered at all.

"I'll tell you if you agree to call me Mack for the rest of the trip when we're not in the conference."

Her lips formed a thin line, and his eyes met hers in challenge. Not wanting to cause any conflict amongst the group, she acquiesced, but she threw him a look that said she would get him back for that.

"Wonderful," he said with a broad smile. "I'd like to see the Museum of Ancient Art and the Porta Palatina. I like to see historical places and things when I'm traveling."

Shar's eyes went wide. She hadn't expected that from him. Her mysterious and demanding surfer didn't seem like the history nerd type. "I'm the same. If I'm traveling, and not on the beach, I like to find the oldest or most scenic places to visit."

"It's settled then!" Tabitha exclaimed, clapping her hands. "I've marked all the places we want to visit on the map, including Garibaldi Street, and then Kevin will find us somewhere to eat lunch at the Central Market." She stood, and Shar followed her lead. Tabitha put her arm around Shar's shoulders and led her toward the main street. "At Garibaldi Street, we can do some shopping, and the guys can sit around and talk shop if they'd like." Her tone was secretive, like she had a plan that required them to be away from the men. Shar smiled and nodded in agreement.

The sights, sounds, and food were absolutely amazing, and Shar couldn't have asked for a better day. She learned so much about her companions on their waking tour. Kevin was so in love with his wife, that he would do anything she asked. Any questions he asked or complaints he made were more for Shar and Mack's benefit than genuine discomfort. While they enjoyed the park, the couple walked ahead of them. Mack whispered that Kevin had grown up in a house where his parents insisted that outsiders should see the man as the decision-maker regardless of what happened behind closed doors. Tabitha had been trying to help him work through that conditioning by challenging him to allow her a partner's voice in public situations.

"That explains the awkward challenges and petty discussions. I thought maybe they didn't spend much time together outside of the house and wondered what their dynamic was when they were alone," she had responded.

"They are so good to and for each other. Kevin and I have

been friends since we were kids, and I have never seen him so happy." Shar looked at the rest of the couple's interactions from a new perspective the rest of the day.

She and Mack fell into a companionable pattern of pointing out interesting sites and discussing the influence of the ancient art they saw on modern day. Often, they found themselves alone when the happy couple would wander off with their arms around each other.

"Ugh, they're so sickeningly sweet together," she commented one time when Tabitha stood in front of a statue for a photo, and then Kevin leaned in to kiss her while taking the selfie.

"No need to be jealous, Ms. Maxwell. I could put my arm around your shoulder if you'd like."

She cut him a scathing look. He shrugged with a laugh before walking off. She did want him to put his arm around her, and it killed her that he knew it.

When they got to Garibaldi Street, Tabitha dropped her husband's arm and grabbed Shar's. "How about we all meet back here at the street entrance in an hour?"

"What are you up to, Tabs?" Kevin asked her.

"Girl stuff," she said with a laugh and pulled Shar away.

They quickly walked around a couple of outside stalls, out of view of the guys thanks to all the people, and Shar pulled her to a stop. "What are we doing? Do I get to know?"

Tabitha's eyes were shining. "Every time Kevin travels, especially out of the country, he brings me back something that he says reminds him of me, or sometimes it's something naughty he wants to use with me," she said, bumping her shoulder into Shar's. "I want to return the favor, but I can't do that with him standing over my shoulder."

"Why not just do it tomorrow or another day when we're all stuck in the conference?" Shar asked. That seemed like a much better solution than trying to lose the guys on a single street.

"What, and miss the chance of shopping with a friend? Anyway," Tabitha said, pulling Shar toward the back of the market, "Kevin will ask me to stay close to the hotel when he's not available to be my bodyguard."

Shar laughed. She couldn't picture Kevin as the pitbull type. Now Mack, on the other hand. She'd already seen him in action.

"Seriously. He's protective, and it's so sweet, so I don't push it too far."

Shar put her hands up to placate her new friend. "So what type of gift do you want to get?" She asked Tabitha while they walk between stalls and outside of the small storefronts.

"Lingerie," she said decisively.

"For him to wear?"

"No, silly. Wait, what kind do you think they might have?"

Both women laughed. Shar pulled Tabitha to a halt and pointed. Less than 40 yards from them was what appeared to be a lingerie store. Tabitha squealed and almost took off running. They wandered around the store, and Tabitha tried on a couple of body suits before opting for a beautiful lace number that hugged her small frame perfectly, giving her the illusion of an hourglass shape.

"Don't you want to get something? I'm sure you have someone to wear it for," Tabitha said with an expectant look.

Shar weighed telling her new friend about the situation with Mack and that she hadn't been with anyone else since that all fell apart, but she wasn't ready to be that intimate yet. Instead, she found a couple pieces to try on herself.

"Holy shit, girl! That is why your ass is the model and not

me. Your curves are to die for, and that green plays so well with the green in your eyes."

Shar beamed at her friend. She had a hard time keeping female friends because they were either scathing in their comments about her size or envious to the point of making every conversation uncomfortable. Though Tabitha's comment about her not being built for modeling was a bit self-deprecating, she didn't feel any hint of envy from the woman, and Shar could've hugged her. They made their way to the cashier and paid for their purchases.

"Is there anything else you want to look at before we make our way back to the men?" Shar asked.

"No, not really. I'm actually getting tired and may suggest we take a taxi back to the hotel."

"Really? Are you feeling alright?"

Tabitha looked askance, and Shar pulled her to a stop in between a couple of stalls. She stared at her new friend with what she hoped was her best concerned mother look. She didn't have much experience with that look herself, but she'd seen it with Jerry's mother, especially before he and Geoffrey got married.

"Look, you can't say anything, even to Mack, ok?"

Shar's face dropped before she could control it. "You're not sick, are you? We just met, but I was hoping we could be good friends."

Tabitha laughed. "No, nothing like that. I just haven't told my husband that he's going to be a father yet." She was smiling so brightly that Shar couldn't help but smile back.

"Oh shit, you're pregnant?"

Tabitha nodded. "I just found out last week, and I knew that if I told Kevin, he wouldn't have brought me. Remember what I said about protective? I'm going to put on this lingerie while I can still fit in it and tell him while I ride him."

"Well, that's one way to do it," Shar said, fully supporting her choice. It sounded like something she'd do if she ever decided to have children.

"Please don't say anything."

Shar gestured turning a key in front of her lips and grabbed her friend's arm. "Let's go find Poppa Kev."

"Shhh," Tabitha reprimanded, giggling all the way to where the men were standing.

"Did you ladies find everything you were looking for," Mack asked when they got close enough.

"For now," Tabitha said before Shar could say anything. The woman took her husband's outstretched hand and leaned in for him to kiss her temple. "Can we get a taxi back to the hotel?" she asked, looking up into Kevin's eyes. He gave her a concerned look, but when she simply said she was tired from all the walking, he smiled and walked to the street to hail a cab.

"I think I'd rather walk," Shar said, watching his attempts and the way people were driving.

Tabitha's look said she was about to argue that it wasn't safe for Shar to walk back alone. Never having been one to concern herself with potential dangers when traveling, Shar was already prepared with her own argument that she'd be fine when Mack chimed in.

"I'd be glad to walk back with you, if you wouldn't mind the company."

Shar was about to deny him the opportunity when Tabitha visibly relaxed and smiled at the insufferable man. She wouldn't have Tabitha worrying on her behalf or feeling the stress of arguing when it wasn't necessary. To spare her friend, Shar thanked him. They both walked Tabitha to where Kevin was talking with the cabbie, and they said their goodbyes with a promise to grab breakfast together before the conference started.

"You really didn't have to play bodyguard. I've traveled alone many times."

Mack laughed. "Is that what you think I'm doing? I assure you, it is not."

"No? What is it then?"

"If I said that I had to keep our secret weapon safe, you'd call me an ass and probably never talk to me again, so I won't do that."

Shar stopped in the middle of the sidewalk and turned to stare at him, hands on her hips. He stopped and matched her stance.

"Don't be an ass, Mack, and I won't call you one."

"Really, I didn't want to ride back alone with the lovebirds. They were all over each other today, and I didn't want to be a third wheel. Besides, tomorrow is their anniversary, and I have him out here working."

Remembering the news Tabitha shared with her and the couple's obvious affection, Shar softened her look a bit. She believed him. She really didn't want to ride back with them either.

"Tabitha didn't tell me it was their anniversary, just that she wanted to get something special for Kevin." She turned and started walking again.

"Oh yeah?" he asked with a mischievous lilt to his voice. "What did she get?"

"I'm not supposed to tell," she said with a smile, while increasing the speed of her step to stay out of the range of his arms. She turned her head back to see him eyeing her predatorily. Her heart rate increased, and heat flowed through her.

"Is this some girl code thing?" His footsteps gained on her, and she weighed her options. Did she start running and make it look like he was chasing her for real, or did she let him catch her. At the next corner, though, she realized she didn't know which direction to turn for their hotel. Kevin and Tabitha had been leading the way all day. She stopped and waited for Mack to catch up. He seemed to be breathing normally, while she had been working to catch her breath from their power walk. "Do you know which way we have to turn to get back to the hotel from here?"

He looked left and right down the cross street and then back the way they had come. "Um, I'm not sure. Let's see if I can get a signal for the GPS."

Music streamed from the street to their right. There were what looked to be a few cafes and possibly a bar or two on that road. Drawn by the music, Shar started walking in that direction before Mack had even pulled up the hotel on his phone.

"Hey, where are you going?"

He ran to meet her where she stood outside of the entrance to what appeared to be a small dive bar. She was standing in the short line outside and trying to look through the door. This would be so much easier if she knew Italian. She needed to put more time into those language apps she kept downloading onto her phone and forgetting.

"I think they have live music," she said when he stood at her side. She was swaying to the beat.

"We have an early morning. Do you think this is a good idea?"

"Good? Probably not, but it could be fun!" She followed the line into the bar before yelling over her shoulder, "You coming?"

CHAPTER 27
MACK

Mack could think of about fifty other things he'd rather do than spend the evening in a bar, but the look on her face said she wasn't taking no for an answer. Even if he left her, she was still going to go in and listen to the music. He thought back to the night he'd followed her around to the different bars on the island. She'd had a good time until that last one, or at least she was able to look like she was having a good time. That's the only reason he hadn't approached her at any of the others. This time, though, she wasn't here with anyone else, and she invited him to join her. Taking a deep breath, he entered the establishment.

The place was much bigger on the inside than it looked. There were two bars once you passed through a long hallway. This was his first time in Turin, so he wasn't sure what to expect from their nightlife. Hell, her rarely went out at home. There was no bouncer at the door patting anyone down, nor was he stopped to pay a cover charge. The main bar was near the entrance, and there were wine bottles lined up from the counter to the ceiling on either side of the liquor stands. In the back of the large open room was a stage with a trio playing music. The lyrics were in Italian, but the melody sounded familiar. He really needed to work on his mastery of Italian. This was his fourth time to the country, and his abilities were still poor.

He looked around the room trying to catch sight of the beautiful woman he'd followed inside. When he didn't see here right away, his pulse raised, and his eyes darted back and forth, searching the dance floor, the bar area, and the small groups standing in front of the stage. He was going to choke her for real for disappearing on him. Then a hand landed on his shoulder.

"I wasn't sure if you were going to come in or not."

"I wasn't going to leave you when you still didn't know how to get back to the hotel."

"Is that really the reason?" she asked, and he caught the incredulity in her voice.

"It's a reason."

She laughed, and he turned back in her direction. "Can we call a truce, at least for tonight. We can just be two colleagues hanging out before the big meeting."

He wasn't sure he'd heard her right. "A truce? Are we at war?"

"You know what I mean. I don't want to get in trouble with the boss for enjoying myself on a work night. So can we just be Mack and Shar?"

He smirked. "Sure."

"Cool," she said with a smile. "I'm getting a drink." He watched her walk off toward the bar, hips swaying to the beat of the music. Okay, maybe he was just imagining that last part.

She came back with two drinks in her hands, and he raised a brow at her. "Double fisting tonight?"

"I hadn't planned to get lucky, but let me look around the room," she responded without missing a beat.

He blew out a breath. He wanted to grab ahold of her and give her twenty reasons why he wasn't letting anyone else near her, but that would not meet her truce. She held one of the drinks out to him, and he silently took it. She raised the glass she still held toward him, and he tapped his to it, eliciting a smile from her. It was probably the first genuine smile she'd given him since... No, he wasn't going to think about that. He needed to stay in the moment and just be grateful she didn't send him away, though he wouldn't have left her anyway. Whether she liked it or not, he was going to be close enough to step in should she need it. He could be patient when needed.

"There's a table down there," she said, though he hardly heard her over the music that was not streaming through the speakers. The group must've taken a break while she was getting their drinks. He followed her toward the stage where she found an empty table against the wall. "We'll be able to see from here," she said, raising her voice.

Mack nodded and joined her. He moved his seat against the wall, so the table was in front of them rather than between them. She moved her chair back toward the wall as well. He wasn't sure if her intention was to be closer to him, but he wasn't going to ask. She put the bag she had been carrying on the floor between their chairs, and he started to ask what she had bought, but he got distracted watching her sway to the music. It took him back to that night she was dancing, her body like silk. He wasn't much of a dancer himself, but he hated watching her dance with that kid. He imagined putting his arms around her and feeling her glide up and down against his body. He was glad they were seated because his erection was also imagining her body against his.

"You like to dance," he said, more of a statement than a question.

"Yes. I love music and the way the rhythm just flows. I imagine it's kind of like your surfing. You move so fluidly on your board."

"It took years to learn how to ride the waves without falling off or damn near drowning myself. Now, it is the most relaxing thing I know." He stopped himself before adding *except for sex*.

She looked at him intently, and he felt warmth rushing up his neck. She was nodding in agreement, and he wondered if she thought sex was as relaxing as dancing.

"I didn't realize you had watched me so carefully to know how I moved on the board." Her cheeks turned red, and she looked away toward the stage.

"I like watching aesthetically pleasing things. Someone who is good at their craft, or deep in their passions is a sight to behold."

"Agreed," he said, his voice a little huskier than intended.

The crowd around them started clapping as the trio climbed back onto the stage. Shar's attention was now focused there, giving Mack the opportunity to admire her profile. She really was stunning with her long neck, pouty lips, and pert nose. He wouldn't bother to look down at her curves. He could still feel them in his dreams. *Friends, Mack. Colleagues. Just two people hanging out, nothing more. Keep it together.* He chided himself for the way his thoughts were going and tried to focus on the music coming from the stage. Shar was already dancing in her seat.

"Go dance. I can tell you want to," he said, loud enough so she could hear him over the music.

She looked into his eyes for a moment, as if discussing the possibilities with herself before finally getting off the tall chair and making her way to the dance floor. Most of the people out there were coupled up. Some held hands and moved together with twists and turns. Mack assumed it was some kind of local dance because he'd never seen it before and couldn't say what it was called. There were other couples who danced much more tightly together, hands on each other's hips, bodies moving as one. They weren't quite gyrating like he would see at home in the clubs, but they were definitely stuck like glue. And then, there was Shar. Her body moved like butter in a hot pan, hip sliding in one direction, while her torso went in its opposite. Suddenly, everyone in the room went away, and all he could see was her. She spun until she made him dizzy, and her arms stretched out like she was reaching for him. When the music stopped, and she stopped, it took him a couple minutes to stop himself from swaying with her in the trance.

Shar came back to the table and downed the rest of her drink. He, too, finished his off.

"Would you like another?"

She nodded vigorously, and he hopped down from the seat, making his way to the bar. He wasn't sure what she had ordered for them, so he could get the same thing, but he wasn't going back to ask her. Instead, he walked up and looked at their specials. Not knowing exactly what he was ordering, he picked something that the person next to him had ordered. It looked good. When he got back to the table, Shar looked at the drinks in his hands and tilted her head to the side in question. He shrugged with a wry smile and handed one to her. She laughed and took a quick sip. A smile spread across her lips, and she took another sip before putting the glass down on the table. She hadn't taken a seat, instead, she continued moving to the new song.

"You should come dance with me," she said.

"I don't dance," he responded with a definitive shake of his head.

"The way you move on that board and in bed..." Her voice trailed off at that last part, and he wasn't sure he'd heard her correctly. After a second, and two red cheeks, she finished her thought. "I bet you would be a great dance partner."

He laughed. "I'm barely a good business partner, let alone any other kind."

Though he couldn't hear her, he watched her lips tsking at him, and he smiled. She didn't believe him, but he'd never been good at working together fully with someone. He and Kevin had only lasted this long because Kevin was so good at the numbers, and he allowed Mack to take the lead in most business decisions. That's why staying away from the marketing ads, shoots, and meetings had been so hard these past couple months. Who the hell was he lying to? Being a control freak had nothing to do with why these past months were so hard. This woman, this goddess in front of him...she was the reason he had to stay away and the reason every damn day was a struggle. And now here she was inviting him to dance, something he wasn't good at, and he was struggling to say yes.

"Don't get mad if I step all over your toes," he said.

She giggled and held out a hand to him. He looked down at her outstretched fingers and grasped them with his own. Downing his drink, he stepped around the table until he was standing next to her.

"I'm not a porcelain doll you'd just break by stepping on her," she said and then pulled him toward an open area of the floor in front of the stage.

She looked into his eyes and reached her hands around his neck, pulling him down toward her. He held his breath when she brought her mouth to his ear.

"Put your hands on my waist. We'll start slow. Once you get the hang of it, I'll loosen my hold and let you move on your own." She lifted her gaze to his eyes again for a response. He nodded, hoping she couldn't read his uncertainty. "Now, I'm going to sway my hips left and right. You'll feel them with your hands, and I want you to follow with your hips in the same way."

She started moving a little at a time in each direction. It took a few seconds before he caught on, and his body matched hers. Her head was in the space between his neck and shoulder, and he leaned into it, laying his cheek against her hair. It felt so good to hold her, and she smelled divine, just like she had on the plane.

"Now," she said against his ear again, "I'm going to move

my hips in a different motion, and I want you to follow my lead. Think of it like riding the waves. Your body adjusting for the flow of the water. Here, you're adjusting to how I move, allowing your hands to determine what way to go next."

He held onto her, his fingers grasping into her soft middle until he found her rhythm. Slowly, as he caught the wave of her body, they relaxed and splayed against the expanse of her hips. She let out a deep sigh against his neck, and he felt his dick respond. She must have felt it too because she loosened her grip on his neck a little until they were staring into each other's eyes.

She smiled up at him, "I knew you'd have no problem figuring it out. Of course, there are other dances and other types of dancing, but this is simple and matches your skills."

He curled his lip in a smirk, and then she turned in his arms, her back to his chest. His breath caught, as her ass rubbed against him. He immediately released her hips, not knowing what to do next, and she reached back for his hands. Putting them back in place, she slid one arm up around the back of his head, pulling him down, so he could hear her.

"Don't ever let go. Just keep moving."

And he did. His body matching hers, his hands sliding against her body, from her hip to her waist, to her thighs depending on how she moved. She hadn't been lying. This really was like being on a surfboard, and his body relaxed into the rhythm the same as it did on the water. How had he not realized this all these years? He almost missed the end of the band's set until the crowd's applause penetrated his thoughts. The floor was empty except for them, and the only thing he could hear was the hum of conversation around the venue.

"Maybe we should go back to the table," he suggested against her ear.

"Maybe it's time to head back to the hotel," she responded, her voice husky.

He didn't think too much on her words, just nodded and

spun her until he could lead her toward their stuff. She finished off her drink, and he grabbed the bag she'd forgotten when she headed toward the door. She turned around with a panicked look, and he held the bag up to her. With a hand to her chest, she smiled at him and walked back to grab it from his hand.

"Do you still want to walk back or see if we can find a main road and catch a cab?"

"I don't know. Did you ever get to GPS how far we were from the hotel?"

"Someone dashed off, and I didn't get to finish..."

She looked at him with squinted eyes, and he fought hard not to crack a smile.

"That's what she said," Shar blurted, throwing them both into hysterics.

CHAPTER 28

SHAR

S har's eyes went wide. Did she really just say that to him? She swallowed, ready to apologize when he burst out laughing. She followed his lead and doubled over in laughter, putting her hand out and touching his chest to steady herself. A buzz went through her body when his pecs flexed under her palm.

"Let's just forget I said that," she offered once she caught her breath.

A devilish light entered his eyes, and he shook his head. "No ma'am. I can't forget anything you've said. You'd hold it against me somehow."

She pursed her lips and put her hands on her hips. "That's not true. I don't expect you to remember every single thing I've ever said."

"Stand there pouting those lips as much as you want, but if you keep looking at me like that, I may forget our agreement to just be colleagues tonight."

The intensity of his gaze made her mouth go dry. She probably shouldn't push too much if she was not willing to go with him. Oh, who the hell was she lying to, she would go willingly. Hell, she'd lead the charge. She held out her phone and did a quick map search.

Turning her phone, allowing him to see, she said, "We're only a few blocks. Let's walk."

"Lead the way, Ms. Maxwell."

She cut her eyes in his direction. Something about him calling her by her formal name when they've been so casual the past few hours didn't feel right. She headed in the direction of the hotel, her brows furrowed, until he pulled her to a halt with his hand on her waist. She closed her eyes, as she pulled her close, his breath on her neck.

"Put your claws away, Pretty. That wasn't a challenge."

Lifting her hand, she folded her nails down, mimicking a cat retracting their claws, and he chuckled before placing a light kiss on her cheek.

"Thank you."

"For?" she asked after they had walked half a block. She needed the time to get her heartbeat under control. The man made her weak, and it was taking all her willpower not to jump into his arms.

"Huh?"

"What were you thanking me for?"

He didn't answer right away, and Shar looked over her shoulder to make sure he was still walking with her. He looked everywhere but in her direction as they walked, and she wondered what had made him so pensive. He responded before she could ask.

"So much. Thank you for being in my presence today. Thank you for letting me accompany you this evening. Thank you for the dance lesson, and for not shredding me with those claws. Just, thank you for your time."

"I don't hate you, Mack." She stopped in the shadow of a shade tree that covered the part of the sidewalk they were passing. "On the contrary..." she whispered.

He leaned toward her, his ear turned in her direction. It

was obvious he wanted her to repeat what she'd said, but the words caught in her throat. He reached out and rubbed the backs of his knuckles against her cheek, and she leaned into the warmth of his hand. When he turned it to cup her cheek, she reached up and around his neck, pulling his face to hers. The moment their lips touched, her body exploded with need. She sucked on his bottom lip until he opened for her, and when his tongue touched hers, she moaned. His hands reached around to her ass and pulled her tight against him. His need was evident against her stomach, and she shuddered.

"How far are we from the hotel?" he asked, and she laughed, extricating herself from his arms.

Shar entwined her fingers with his and pulled him down the street so quickly he was laughing too.

She stopped for a second. "Hey, where's my bag?" Once again, he lifted it in his hand, and she gave him a sheepish smile. "How'd you? You know what, never mind. Forget I asked that question."

They walked into the hotel hand-in-hand, oblivious of anyone in the lobby or around them. As they waited for the elevator, he snuck up behind her and whispered in her ear.

"I need to tell you something." She made to turn around, but he held her still, sending tremors of anticipation and nerves through her body. "Last night, I heard you call my name."

She froze. What did he mean? Her heart raced with worry that he was outside of her room when she was masturbating. "How?" she asked quietly.

"My room is next to yours. No, don't turn around. Don't be embarrassed. Just listen."

The elevator was taking forever to come back down to the first floor, and he held her tightly against him with one arm. Though her brain told her to step away, her body was trembling with thoughts of him hearing her moans. Shit, he knew she was getting off to thoughts of him. She should have asked for everyone's room number before they all went to bed.

"I was reading the book you were reading on the plane. It's very hot, by the way. And then I heard a whimper through the wall. I thought I'd imagined things until it happened again."

His mouth never left her ear, and she felt every one of his breaths. Shockwaves made their way down her back and around to her core. She was so wet already and his words made her squirm, her body wanting to rub against him. When the elevator started descending again, his hand slid down her abdomen. Thankfully, there was no one else in the hallway with them, else they'd get a show because she was helpless against this spell that was weaving around them.

"Then I heard you talking and had a moment of jealousy I can't even describe. Thankfully, I heard a buzzing sound that accompanied your moans before I tore into your room. My cock nearly jumped out of my pajamas on its own at the sound of you getting yourself off."

His hand was getting increasingly close to the spot she needed him to touch when the elevator doors opened, and a group of people walked past them. Without letting her go, Mack led her into the elevator and pressed the door closed button before their floor. When they started moving, she heard the bag he was holding hit the floor before his other hand was around her, squeezing her breast through her shirt. His hand slid into the waistband of her leggings and found her clit.

"Fuck, Mack, please," she cried.

"Please what? You didn't beg last night, just moaned repeatedly while working that vibrator in and out of you. You had me so fucking hard; I nearly damaged my dick stroking it so fast."

His fingers deftly worked her clit until she couldn't see straight.

"More. I need more."

"Tell me I can have you. Tell me you won't hate me in the morning."

He slid his fingers down to plunge them into her, and she rubbed herself against his palm. Why did he want her to talk? She couldn't even think straight.

"Tell me I can come with you while you scream my name."

Her entire body tensed, and he tightened his arms around her. Her knees tried to buckle, and he held her up.

"Tell me, Shar. We're almost to our floor, and I need to know."

"Yes, fuck, Mack. I need you in me. Tonight, we are just you and me. Tomorrow, you're my boss. Tonight, I just want to forget everything and feel."

Suddenly, he pulled his hand from her pants, and she whimpered. He stepped back from her and was licking his fingers when she looked up at him. A jolt of heat ran through her at the sight. It didn't matter that she'd just come; she wanted him naked and inside of her. He picked up the bag again right before the door opened.

"What did you ladies buy anyway?"

She gave him a sly smile and asked, "Would you like to see?"

"What do you think?"

She reached out and grabbed the bag from him and then took his hand to lead him to her room.

"Mine's closer," he said, trying to stop her on the way.

She barely registered his words and only stopped because of how strongly he pulled on her hand.

"I'm right here, Pretty." He was already opening the door, so she decided not to fight with him about it. It didn't matter where they were, so long as his body was on hers.

His suite was the exact opposite of hers, including where his bed was located. It was no wonder he'd heard her last night. She didn't even want to think about what might've happened had it been someone else listening to her. A shiver ran through her at the thought.

He leaned against the bar stool facing her. There was both lust and worry in his beautiful eyes. She walked between his legs and leaned up to kiss his chin and then his lips once he'd dipped his head.

"I will not hate you tomorrow. I want you. I won't lie; I always want you. I've not stopped thinking about you since that first night. So, yeah, tomorrow will be hard. Every day after will be hard, but tomorrow is not tonight." She held his face between her hands and kissed him deeply. "I'll be right back," she said, picking her bag up and heading toward what she knew was the bathroom from its location opposite her own.

She woke in the morning with her limbs entwined with Mack's. Memories of the previous night's adventures ran through her mind, and her body ached deliciously. Looking over at the alarm clock provided by the hotel, she sighed. It was still early but far too late for her to still be here before emotions came crashing in on her. She tried to slide herself out of the bed without waking him, but it was impossible. His eyes slid open, though it took a few moments before they cleared.

"Hi there, handsome. I need to go back to my room and start getting ready."

"What time is it?"

His voice was still raspy from sleep, and her core thrummed in response. "It's four."

"A.M.? You're leaving so early?"

Though he'd said it as a question, she felt the accusation in his words. "You left me this early before."

His eyes turned sad, and he turned away. "I understand," he said without looking at her again.

She walked around gathering the new lingerie he had thrown around the room as he removed them. Picking up each piece was like picking up pieces of her heart. She felt shattered and exposed. Rather than taking the time to get dressed, she pulled one of his robes from the bathroom and wrapped herself in it. She should have stayed away from him. She had promised Jerry she'd do her best to keep away from him, but damn if she didn't instigate the time they spent together. What the fuck was wrong with her? By the time she walked into her room, tears were running down her face. She flopped on the bed and grabbed her phone to call Jerry.

No sooner had he picked up the call than she blurted, "I fucked up, Jer." Her voice cracked.

"Oh honey. You fucked him, didn't you?"

"He danced with me. He looked in my eyes, and I needed him."

"So, now what?" he asked.

"Can't you just empathize with me? Can't you just be my best friend and let me cry on your shoulder from thousands of miles away?"

"This is me empathizing, Shar. You have three more days there and another 9 months in this contract. You've got to figure out something and quickly."

"I can't stand you and your logic. I just want to cry in a corner, but we have breakfast to attend in just a couple hours."

"And let me guess that he'll be at breakfast."

"Of course! He's the fucking boss."

"You should have remembered that last night."

"You're an asshole!"

"And I love you."

Shar clicked the button to end the call without saying goodbye. She normally appreciated Jerry's no-holds-barred logic, but damn if she didn't need something softer this morning. Instead, she curled up into a ball.

She jumped, heartbeat racing when both her phone rang and someone knocked on the door simultaneously. "What?" she yelled aloud to both the obnoxious sounds.

"Shar, are you alright?" A female voice came through the door.

The voice sounded familiar, but Shar couldn't quite tell. She started to slide out from the middle of the king-size bed, looking at her phone's screen. The call was from Mack. She sent him to voicemail and padded to the door, still wrapped in the robe from his room. Opening the door with the safety lock still on, she peered out to see Tabitha standing in the middle of the hall looking perfectly put together.

"There you are! We were all getting worried."

Shar looked at Tabitha and back towards the phone on her bed. Oh no, what time was it?

"I'm so sorry. I must've fallen back asleep."

"So, open the door and I'll wait while you get ready."

Shar knew she looked like shit. She could feel the puffiness in her eyes and the tightness in her muscles. There was probably mascara running down her face too. Still, she opened the door to the closest person she had to a friend here and gestured for Tabitha to enter.

The other woman took one step inside, looked at her face and quickly closed the door. "Oh my god, honey, what happened to you? Did something happen last night after we came back to the hotel? Mack looked like shit too!"

"No, nothing like that. We made it back safely, though probably later than we should have. I got it in my head to pop into a local bar with live music and hang out. Mack hung out to babysit, and I probably kept him out too late."

"That doesn't explain why you look like you spent the entire night crying."

Shar stared at the woman unsure what to say. Should she tell her the whole story? Make up something? Maybe a horrible accident at home?

"Don't just stare at me. You have to be on stage today. Go fix your face and talk at the same time. How can I help?"

Tabitha's directives were clear and probably the only thing that would have penetrated the haze of confusion and pain that was plaguing Shar right then. She quickly stepped into the bathroom and started the shower. Wrapping her hair into a tight bun, she grabbed a makeup wipe and cleaned the running mascara before jumping into the hot water stream. When she came out of the bathroom wrapped in a towel, Tabitha had already pulled some clothes out of her closet, and Shar made a final decision on what to wear for the day. Not knowing the full itinerary or the amount of walking she'd be doing, Shar opted for a 3-inch pump rather than her normal stilettos. With her undergarments on, she popped back into the bathroom to try and salvage her hair and reapply makeup to cover the puffiness and dark circles below her eyes.

Tabitha leaned against the door jamb watching her. "Now spill it," she said.

Feeling slightly more human that she had the first time her friend asked what happened, Shar decided to take a chance and tell the truth, at least some of it.

"Has Kevin told you anything about when Mack and I first met?" Tabitha shook her head. Shar brushed her hair out until it shined again, and then she added a bit of dry shampoo to help give it some lift at the root. "Well, we have history, and by history, I mean that we met the week before I signed the contract with them."

"Oh?"

Looking at her through the mirror, Shar could tell Tabitha

didn't fully understand what she was saying. "By met, I mean, we hooked up at a hotel in California." Tabitha's eyes grew wide. "We didn't exchange names, and I had no idea I was even being offered a contract by Velocity at the time. My agent told me the next day when I was getting ready to head home." She twisted her hair up into a clip and pulled a few tendrils around her temples. "Anyway, when I got to the east coast, Mack was magically there too, but I still didn't know who he was. I only met Kevin when I signed the contract." It was harder to continue the conversation while putting on her makeup, so she gave Tabitha a few minutes to absorb all that she'd said thus far. Tabitha's face was a mixture of shock and fascination. "We hooked up again and managed to spend the weekend together. It was great, until Monday morning when I went into the first meeting about the marketing plan and who walked through the door as my new boss? The man I'd been fucking and damn near falling for."

"Oh shit!"

"Oh shit, indeed." She pointed the mascara wand in Tabitha's direction. "I have one rule. I don't fuck where I work. No coworkers and definitely no bosses. My career is too important to me for that, and there are too many men readily available."

Tabitha nodded in ready agreement. "One day, I'll tell you how Kevin and I got together," she said chuckling. For now, though, I'm still waiting to find out what had you looking so miserable when you opened the door this morning."

"Well, when I found out Mack was Sloan Mackenzie, my boss, I was pissed. I told him to go fuck himself and to never approach me. Problem was, like I said, I was already falling for him. Somehow, though, we managed to stay out of each other's way for the better part of the past couple months..."

"Until this trip," her friend added.

"Yeah. Needless to say, we should have just come back to the hotel with you two last night because we would have gone our separate ways instead of me waking up in his bed at four this morning. The tears were from the regret of having to leave and go back to having this wall between us because he's my fucking boss, and I didn't fucking know." Her voice cracked, and she waved her hands in front of her face trying to dry her makeup before the tears bubbled free.

"No, ma'am, you do not have time for crying or to redo your beautiful face." Tabitha handed her a bottle of water from the mini fridge. "Let's go get us some breakfast and help you make it through the day. I was going to find somewhere quiet to read my book, but I think you need a buffer between you and Mack, especially if my husband is failing in that job." Tabitha opened her arms and Shar walked into them. "Everything will be fine. Contracts aren't forever."

"You know, my agent and best friend told me that same thing when all of this first went down."

"Oh," Tabitha said right as they entered the elevator, "I told Kevin about the baby last night, so if he hasn't already told Mack and decides to share, please act surprised."

"I got you."

CHAPTER 29

MACK

"Man, why did you let us stay out together last night?"

"You're not blaming me for that, man. You both are grown ass people. You were supposed to walk back to the hotel. That was it!"

"That's what we were doing until we got turned around and she found a bar with live music. We drank, and she taught me how to dance." He slammed his fist down on the table, and the glassware shook.

"Calm down, dude. We are here for a conference and do not need these people thinking you are out of your damn mind."

"I feel like I'm losing my mind. This woman makes me crazy. She makes me feel. I don't know what to do with these feelings."

"Nine more months, dude. That's it. The contract is over in nine more months."

Mack shook his head. Nine months felt like forever when he could still smell her all around him, even after his shower. Her scent permeated the room, and the taste of her skin was stuck on his tongue.

"Speaking of nine months," Kevin said, the wistful shift in his voice catching Mack's attention. "The reason Tabitha wanted to come back to the hotel last night was to give me my anniversary gift." Mack raised a brow and smirked. "Shut up, Mack. If I can listen to you whine about your sex life, you can hear about mine too, dammit. Anyway, that wasn't my only gift."

Kevin looked up, his facing lighting up at whatever or whoever he saw. Mack turned around to see Tabitha and Shar walking into the restaurant. Kevin jumped up and took his wife's hand, leading her to the table, but all of Mack's attention was on Shar's approach. She didn't even look at him, and though she took the empty seat to his right, she never turned his way. His heart sunk lower.

"Good morning, ladies," he said, hoping to at least get her attention for a second.

"I just left you not that long ago, Mack. I actually woke poor Shar up. She had missed her wakeup call."

And she ignored mine, Mack thought, managing to keep from saying the words aloud. He went to open his mouth and speak to Shar directly when Kevin spoke again.

"So, as I was saying, and now that we're all here together, Tabitha gave me the best anniversary gift ever."

Shar looked up at the couple, and Mack pried his eyes away from her to attend to his friend's story. Kevin took Tabitha's hand up on the table, and he looked as though, no, that couldn't be right. There were tears in Kevin's eyes. Mack hadn't seen his friend cry since their wedding, and before that, he'd only seen it at his parents' funeral. What was happening. He glanced in Shar's direction, and she was smiling. Did she already know?

Tabitha put her hand over their clasped hands. "What my husband is trying to say is that we will be having a baby in about seven months."

Mack nearly knocked over his chair jumping out of it.

"What? That's amazing!" He went around the table and hugged the couple from behind, kissing them both on the cheeks. "Holy shit, I'm going to be an uncle!" His eyes flipped up to Shar, and she had covered her mouth. Her eyes couldn't lie, though, and there was laughter in them. She had known and was laughing at his surprise.

"I'm so happy for you both," she said.

"Thank you, Shar," both Kevin and Tabitha responded in unison. "And thank you, Uncle Mack," Tabitha told him, looking over her shoulder. "Now, you can return to your seat and stop being a spectacle for the rest of the restaurant," Kevin said, looking around with feigned embarrassment, as the smile never left his face.

"This calls for a toast," Mack said, signaling for the server.

"None for me," Tabitha reminded him.

"Don't worry. I got you." He ordered three regular mimosa and one made with sparkling grape juice. Though he hadn't thought about it before asking, he was kind of surprised they had it readily available. If they hadn't, he'd have asked them to suggest something else they could make without alcohol.

Once they had done their celebration and eaten breakfast, Kevin offered to walk Tabitha back to the room before meeting Mack and Shar in their first session. Mack was taken aback when she declined the offer and said she'd be accompanying them to serve as moral support for Shar.

"She's never been to one of these, and it's easier to stand in front of a crowd like that with a friend in the audience. Since you two are both her bosses, you cannot serve as her friend."

Mack felt like he'd been pierced through the chest at her insinuation. Had Shar told Tabitha about them? Of course, if she really did feel alone and like she needed a friend, it would make sense that she had shared the situation with the other woman. Dammit, he hoped Tabitha didn't think poorly of him because of it. He didn't need two women snubbing him for the next three days.

Throughout the day, and the next two days, Mack made attempts to engage Shar in idle conversation. He didn't even care if they talked about what was between them. He simply wanted to hear her voice talking to him, maybe hear her laughter. That would have been a wonderful gift. Somehow, she managed to evade his attempts at every turn, and when they'd finally go back to their rooms, she'd either rush off early or hang out with Tabitha until after he'd left. He'd considered waiting for her in the hallway right outside of the elevator on their floor, but he didn't want to make things worse when she was actively avoiding him. It's not like he didn't know why and hadn't agree to those parameters. He hadn't been thinking straight when he'd made that agreement, and he regretted it more than anything. They should have just left things as they were because now it all felt so much harder.

The convention went off without a hitch. Every one of their presentations and panels were well-received. They walked away with leads for several international investors who would be willing to help them expand beyond the U.S., and preorders for the Version 2 had quadrupled. Shar was the catalyst for that last bit of growth. She really sold the product. It helped that she was able to pull her own Version 2 from her pocket and show them what it could do. Kevin's last-minute idea to give Shar and that other model their own phones with lifetime upgrades was brilliant. She'd had long enough with the device to have put it through the paces of everyday use. This sold it to the tech junkies and family leaders who were looking for lesser-known devices to use as clout or for their children/spouses. It was a big win for Velocity.

Though Shar had agreed to a celebratory dinner the last

night they were in Turin, she remained aloof to him, giving most of her attention to Tabitha. While he was glad the women had hit it off, he still had an uneasy feeling that their prolonged friendship might make things difficult for him and Kevin. The only thing that could make this situation worse for him was if Shar also made friends with Janet. He would never hear the end of it at that point, and he'd just have to quit the company altogether and become a beach bum. That thought made him smile for a second, remembering that's what Shar had thought of him when they first met. His smile died when Tabitha and Shar walked out of the hotel toward the hired car arm-in-arm. How had the pendulum swung so profoundly for him over the course of a week?

The flight was just as uncomfortable as their meals had been. Kevin wasn't even good for conversation, opting to sleep most of the flight home. Once again, Tabitha and Shar exchanged devices, so they were both focused on their books. Again, Shar had turned away from him toward the window, so he took the time to read over her shoulder. It was another romance. How did she read those things regularly? He had finished the book she read on the way to Italy, and while it was good, he couldn't imagine reading them one right after the other. Yet, there was nothing else to do, so he read along with her.

He didn't last very long. The first sex scene had him thinking about the night they had spent together. The discomfort in his pants matching the pain in his chest at her emotional distance was more than he could bear. He wanted to reach out and touch her shoulder, play in her hair, or pull her into his lap, but he couldn't. Nine fucking months. How the fuck was he supposed to make it nine fucking months?

Pulling out his own phone, he scrolled through his contacts, trying to think of what he'd have done before he met her to relieve these unwanted feelings. As soon as he passed the entries for April and Mona, he blew out a breath. He had no interest in either one of them, nor the other women he'd known over the years. It's not that they weren't beautiful or didn't satisfy him sexually. They just never got beyond his walls. He was able to keep them at arm's length. Somehow, Shar broke through, and now that she was in, he didn't know what to do or how to behave around her. He was trying so hard to respect her boundaries, or rather the one fucking boundary that kept them apart, but damn if it wasn't killing him to do so.

Their arrival back on the east coast was anticlimactic. Shar said her goodbyes to Tabitha with hugs and promises to call. She again congratulated Kevin and told him to take care of his wife. Then she turned to him and congratulated him on a successful conference. What the fuck was that? He started to tell her to shove her congratulations, but she'd already turned away and was heading off to her departure gate to go home. He still wasn't sure where she lived, and he'd stopped himself multiple times from looking up her contract for the contact information. It was enough that he had her phone number, and she ignored his texts. He was not going to make a fool of himself showing up at her door and having her slam it in his face. He watched her walk away until she was out of sight, hoping she'd turn around and at least wave, before he followed his friends to pick up their luggage. She hadn't looked back.

CHAPTER 30
SHAR

The flight back to Housington was never-ending. She tried to focus on her audiobook, but it was impossible. She read Mack into every scene, and her heart shattered all over again. It was so hard not to wrap herself around him before she left, and it took all her strength to walk away without looking back. By the time her plane landed, she had worked herself into such an emotional frenzy that she called Geoffrey instead of a cab. He and Jerry were there by the time she'd collected her luggage. They both wrapped her in their arms, and her tears flowed.

"I don't want to go home alone," she said between sniffles.

Neither one of her friends said anything. They simply piled her bags into the trunk and took her back to their house. Though they had two extra bedrooms, Shar never slept in either one. Her favorite place in their house was in front of the giant fish tank they had in the den. When she walked into the room, she saw there were already pillows and a blanket set out for her. She gave them each a sad smile and curled up on the huge sectional, pulling her feet up under her.

Geoffrey handed her a shot glass, and she downed it

without question. He poured another, and she took that one too. The warmth penetrated the pain, and she took a deep breath. At that point, he returned the bottle to the liquor cabinet and came to sit on the couch next to Jerry. Shar watched the fish swim back and forth, allowing their languid movement to wash over her with a sense of calm. The two men watched over her, as they always did, hands clasped together.

"The trip was great," she said quietly. "Really, it was." The last part came out on a sob, but she pushed past it. I made a new friend, a girlfriend." When both of their brows shot up, she shook her head. "Kevin Dulaney brought his wife with him on the trip. She's wonderful. I really like her, and she helped me make it through the last three days by being a buffer between me and Mack." She fell silent again.

The men looked at each other, and Jerry passed her glass to Geoffrey who started to get up. Shar waved him off. She didn't need another drink. She really hadn't needed the first two, though she did appreciate them.

"I'm okay. I mean, I'm not, but I will be. I've already been through this the first time, right? It's only been a couple months. You'd think that I'd have held the memory of that anger and pain long enough to not make the same mistake already, but that's not how these things work, I guess."

"Hey," Jerry said, "I'm sorry I..."

"No need, Jer. I know what you were trying to do and why, and you weren't wrong. I wasn't ready to hear that the other day, but you weren't wrong."

She reached out and clasped his hand. She'd known Jerry for so long that she could not stay mad at him ever. Everything he did for her was always with good intentions, and she believed that wholeheartedly.

"Was your new friend a better friend than I was?" Jerry asked, concern evident in his voice.

"She was there with me and able to be the friend I needed there. You will never be replaced." She smiled at him, and after a few moments, he returned her smile.

Geoffrey spoke, interrupting the moment. "Okay, now that my husband has made this evening about himself, tell us what you're thinking and feeling about this Mack guy at this moment. We can talk about your new friend later when you are back to being your cheerfully independent self."

Shar laughed. It wasn't a full, belly laugh, but it felt good. She loved that these two men balanced each other out and that they both loved her. She wouldn't make it through life without them.

"I think that if I think too much about him, I forget that I'm supposed to stay away from him. I think he's great. He's funny and sexy, and we like a lot of the same things. He listens and remembers things I've said. As much as I hate this situation between us, I appreciate that he's tried to respect my wishes and stay away. The fact that we were together earlier this week was far more my fault than his. Once I made the first move, though, he ensured I couldn't say no. We're explosive, you know? I don't want to be apart from him, but I can't be around him."

"That's a difficult place to be, love," Geoffrey said, empathy oozing through his expression and voice. "If there was some major boundary that kept me from being with my man here..." He grabbed Jerry's hand again and kissed the back of it. "I don't think that I'd have been able to stay away, especially not when we're put in the same space for days, even hours."

Jerry smiled at him, and Shar's heart melted. She wanted a love like this. Wait, she'd never wanted to be in love before, let alone be with one person. That wasn't in the cards for her, at least that's what she'd always believed.

"What's the matter?" Jerry asked, his face a mask of concern.

Her eyes wide, she shook her head. "I want what you two have. I want a love like yours."

"Girl, who are you, and what have you done with my best friend?"

She stood and looked out the patio door. "I never thought it was possible, but when I'm with him, there is nowhere else I'd rather be, no one I'd rather be with. I'm content in a way I've never been before."

"Does he feel the same way?" Geoffrey asked.

That was a great question. None of this would matter if he wasn't on the same page. But how could she know for sure? She didn't know exactly what he was feeling.

"I...I think so. He acts like it, but we've never talked about our feelings. Truthfully, I probably shouldn't feel this way already. We'd barely just met when I cut him off, and though I've been working for Velocity these past three months, I've hardly seen him until this week. True feelings don't build this fast, do they?"

"When it's right," Geoffrey started. "You just know," Jerry finished.

"But what can I do? I can't just go and say fuck my boundary and my career."

"No, you cannot just throw your career away for some dick, even good dick, when you're not even sure of his feelings toward you. So, what you need to do is figure out his feelings." Jerry said, and she scoffed.

"How the fuck am I supposed to do that when every time we spend any significant time alone together, we can't keep our hands off of each other?"

"Let's sleep on it, and come up with a plan," Geoffrey offered, and they all agreed.

Shar's dreams that night were all about Mack. In one, he professed his love. In the next, he married someone else. Restful sleep was not her friend that night.

The next four months passed in a revolving door blur of advertising shoots and downtime she dreaded. Each time she had to fly out to Wrighton Springs, tension hung in the air as she waited for Mack to make an appearance either at the office, at the shoot, or at her hotel. He had to know she was there, didn't he? It didn't matter that she'd made a plan to avoid him at all costs. She still wondered where he was. Anxiety was getting the best of her, as she imagined him having found someone else or at the very least determined she wasn't worth the hassle.

Days and weeks spent alone in Housington were almost unbearable. Too much time in her own head had never been healthy, and the fact she couldn't depend on any of her coping mechanisms wasn't helping. Every time she asked, no begged, Jerry to find her a gig, there was a reason why it wouldn't work. Most of those reasons revolved around something she had to do for Velocity. The original year's itinerary did not have that many events on it, but damned if Kevin hadn't managed to add enough to have her out of town at least twice monthly. She couldn't even get laid. She'd tried. She'd gone out to a few of the local bars, though she hated hooking up with guys in her town. As soon as she'd get close to going home with someone, though, a smell or sound or touch would remind her of Mack, and she'd be on her way home...alone.

The only positive was spending time with Tabitha whenever she was on the east coast. Her friend was absolutely glowing, and her growing belly bump was the cutest thing. Though Tabitha lamented being pregnant at 34, Shar could tell she was ecstatic about the chance at being a mom. When she saw Kevin with his wife, there was no doubt that the child would be loved and protected beyond measure. He could not wait to be a father, and they were already talking about him taking time off from work to be home after the baby was born. It was a beautiful thing to watch.

More than once, Shar sat with Geoffrey talking about Tabitha and the baby while Jerry was off with one of his other clients.

"After the childhood I had with my mother, I never imagined having kids. Truthfully, I was afraid I'd make the same mistakes for not having any other model."

"Honey, you are not your mother," he'd remind her.

"I know. Logically, I know, but it's hard to feel different when I acknowledge that I've never had a long-term relationship either, just jumping from hook up to hook up."

"By choice. There's a big difference in living your life, embracing your sexuality and loving the way your body works, and being forced into sex work and having your body used for others' pleasure. Your mom made a lot of bad decisions where you were concerned, and for herself as well, but that doesn't mean you would become her simply by getting pregnant."

"Why don't you and Jerry have a kid, so I can just be a happy aunt?"

"We've talked about adopting or getting a surrogate. Then we look at all the older kids who need love and a home. We've even thought of fostering, but there's this fear, you know, that either the system or the kid won't accept us as we are."

They'd held each other more than once when these conversations would happen, tears streaming for all the what ifs. Life was so fucked sometimes.

Then her thoughts would turn to the what ifs about Mack, and the fact she still hadn't seen him. He'd not even attended the same events she had. Kevin wasn't as charismatic as Mack, and that left the selling to her. When she'd ask why Mack hadn't been there, Kevin would shrug and claim a scheduling conflict had them splitting the load. She wasn't sure she bought that excuse, but there was nothing else for her to go on. Mack was obviously avoiding her, and it was making her crazy.

CHAPTER 31

MACK

t had been four months. Four frustratingly long months since he'd done any event travel or been able to get close to Shar. Kevin argued it was better this way.

"I can't keep doing this!" Mack bellowed one evening while they sat in his office going over sales reports.

"Things are going so well, man. She's doing a phenomenal job at every show, and the two of you together right now would just blow all we've worked for out of the water."

"I don't give a fuck. No, seriously, I couldn't care less. I get your point. I do. I've been listening to it for months now with the promise that once this contract is over, we can try to make it work, but what if she fucking forgets about us, about me."

Mack was pacing back and forth in his office by this time, and Kevin just sat there shaking his head.

"There's no way that's happened. She's asked about you at every event. She tries to pry information out of my wife each chance she gets. You're both fucking annoyingly obsessed with each other and yet stubborn as hell."

Mack stood still and cocked his head to the side. "Does she really ask about me?"

"Well, actually, she accuses me of being horrible at public speaking..."

"She's not wrong."

"Ass. And then she thinks I'm lying when I tell her you have other events to attend."

"She's also not wrong."

"She thinks you're purposely avoiding her."

Mack sat in one of the armchairs and downed the bourbon he'd poured twenty minutes earlier. He didn't want her thinking the worst of him. He liked the idea that she still looked for him and asked about him, but how could she even imagine he was avoiding her. Well, he was avoiding her, but not by choice. "Dammit!" He slapped his hand on the table.

"It's almost over, Mack. Just a couple more months."

Kevin then changed the subject just like every other time Mack would fly off the handle. It didn't even make any sense that he'd become so incensed about this woman. It made no sense he couldn't just bury himself in someone else to ease the tension. None of it made any sense, but here he was listening to the description of the next photo shoot she was scheduled for and whether her co-star, who was really nothing more than a side character at this point, would be with her. If she was doing the ads alone, he felt much more relaxed, often pretending they weren't happening and staying away on those days. If that fake-French-speaking guy was around, Mack made it a point to watch from the sidelines, out of her line of vision. Every time that guy stood near Shar or touched her, Mack seethed, but he managed to keep himself from interrupting.

"So, the next shoot will be her alone, and then the grand finale will be a series of still and video shots of them in various intimate poses in and out of a Raven we've leased for the day."

"They'll be in a car together? What do you mean by intimate?"

Kevin closed his eyes with a sigh, and Mack's nostrils flared.

"Look man, it's the very last ad shoot. It's one day, and it'll all be over."

"What do you mean by intimate?"

"I'll send you the specifics when I get them from the videographer."

Mack poured himself another drink.

"Stop drinking that shit, else you'll have to call David to drive you home."

"Or I'll just sleep on the couch. Won't be the first time."

"Well, I'm going home."

"Give Tabs my love."

"Tell her yourself when you come to the baby shower. You are coming, right?"

"Of course, man. Wouldn't miss it!"

Kevin left, and Mack let out an audible groan. He looked at the couch, downed his drink and prepared for the long, uncomfortable night.

The number of times Mack drove up and down the island the past two days just to pass her hotel was ridiculous. He, honestly, could have been called a stalker had anyone paid him any attention. The fact he hadn't walked through the lobby with his board just for the possibility of a chance sighting should get him some credit. It had officially been nearly five months since Italy. Not a word. Not a glance. Nothing. He'd listened to Kevin. He'd lived vicariously through his friend's interactions with Shar. He'd died a little more each night knowing she, too, had distanced herself from him. This obsession had to end.

When he could no longer put off leaving the island, knowing that she should be back at the hotel after the photo shoot, he turned his car toward Kevin and Tabitha's house. He'd never understand why they'd chosen to live inland when there was the possibility of living where the sound of the waves could soothe you to sleep. Of course, he'd not been able to sleep in months. Still, he'd tried to convince Kevin to be his neighbor, but his logical friend insisted his concerns about hurricane season were far more important than a view. So, Mack made the thirty-minute drive to their house and was surprised to see the driveway and street lined with cars.

Mack had forgotten the fact that, though his and Kevin's respective parents were long gone, Tabitha still had strong connections to her parents and extended family. It had taken Kevin a long time to work through his misgivings about family ties. In fact, it was probably the one thing that kept the man from proposing the first month they'd met. Mack left the car with a huge smile on his face at the memory and an even larger gift in his hands. He would not be outdone by her family or any other friends the couple might have. Uncle Mack was going to spoil the hell out of this kid.

Of course, his intentions were overrun as soon as he entered the house and was ushered to the back yard with 'the men'. He'd hardly had the chance to give Tabitha a kiss on the cheek. Kevin gave him an apologetic half smile from across the yard when he got outside. There were only four other men out there, including old man Charlie from the fish and chips shop.

"Hey, Charlie," Mack said in greeting. "I didn't expect to see you here."

Charlie chuckled. "Janet came by the shop the other day and told me to buy a gift because I was coming to celebrate the new addition to the company."

"She did, did she?"

Mack squinted his eyes trying to read the man's

expression. Not that he was surprised by Janet's boldness or her directive, more that he was surprised Charlie would just choose to attend a baby shower for some regular patrons. There had to be more to the story. Still trying to solve the mystery in his head, Mack stepped over and clasped his best friend on the shoulder, pulling him in.

"What's with Charlie and Janet?" he asked, keeping his voice low.

"If you'd have paid more attention to the comings and goings around the office these past couple months instead of wallowing, you'd have known they're now an item."

Mack looked back at the old man and smiled. It was about damn time. Then he registered Kevin's jab at his own behaviors and winced. He'd wanted to argue that he hadn't been wallowing or unaware, but he obviously had been because he had no clue things had progressed between Charlie and Janet.

"Let's not talk about me today and just celebrate you and Tabitha."

Cheers rang out around the small group. Mack made himself a drink and took a seat. It was going to be a long afternoon if they were to be stuck outside all day while all the fun happened inside. He barely got the thought out, though, when Shar came to the door and invited the men inside for food. Mack froze at the sound of her voice before he even turned to see her face. His palms grew sweaty, and he nearly dropped his glass.

"Breathe," Kevin said, clasping his hand on Mack's shoulder before walking into the house.

Mack turned around in time to see Kevin say something to Shar in the doorway. She turned her attention on Mack when he disappeared inside.

"Are you coming inside to eat, or are you just going to stay out here by yourself?"

It was the 'by yourself' that got him moving like a dare. He took the deck stairs two at a time until he was standing within arm's length of her.

"Good afternoon, Ms. Maxwell. I assume your shoot went well this morning?"

He didn't know why he mentioned work. He knew it would do nothing more than remind her of their situation, but he was hoping for some sort of reaction, and he got it.

"The shoot was perfect as always. It was obvious that Velocity spared no expense in its preparation, and I'm grateful for your generosity, Mr. Mackenzie."

The glare in her eyes and the flare of her nostrils was beautiful. If their situation had been any different, the defiant way she said his name would have earned her a thorough spanking, but he was determined to keep his hands to himself until she was ready. He had long-since broken his golden rule of not getting involved. He'd been involved damn near since the first time he'd seen her on that chaise, skin glowing in the sun. There was no point in lying to himself about it now.

"Are we just going to stand here and let all the bugs in?" she asked, her sarcasm scathing.

He gestured for her to lead the way. "After you."

She stomped down the hall, and he took a moment to watch her walk away before following, making sure to pull the door securely closed. The rest of the party was spent watching her try to stay as physically far away from him as possible. It would've been funny if he were watching and not on the receiving end of her snubs. Toward the end of the night, as the house began to empty, he saw her walk toward the basement after finding the hallway bathroom locked. He waited a few seconds and then followed down the stairs. When she exited the bathroom, she nearly plowed into him where he was standing outside of the door.

She screeched and then smacked his chest. "Jesus Christ, Mack! You scared the shit out of me!"

He grabbed her hands. "I thought you weren't afraid of me."

Attempting to take a step back while he held her hands against his chest, she stammered, "I...I'm...I'm not."

His eyes locked on hers. "I can't tell. Your pupils are huge. Your breathing is erratic. And, I'm pretty sure that if I listened closely enough, I could hear your heart racing."

She tried yanking her hands from his, but he held them in place. When she tried backing up again, he stepped with her, pushing her back against the wall.

"I'm not afraid of you, Mack," she said in a whisper. "I just wasn't expecting you to be here."

He choked out a laugh. "Same. And yet, here we both are."

Shar didn't say a word, just stared into his eyes. What was she looking for? Was she hoping to see into his soul? The thought made him bitter. All she'd had to do was ask, and he'd have bared it for her.

"Why have you spent all afternoon avoiding me?" he asked, his face grim.

"Me? You're asking me why I stayed away from you today when you spent the past five months avoiding me?"

"Yes, I am."

"You first," she said, her tone issuing a challenge he was ready to answer with his own.

Desire like he'd not felt before ran through him, and in a voice he hardly recognized, he said, "Because I didn't trust myself to not do this," and pressing her hands against the wall on either side of her head, he kissed her.

This wasn't a slow, passionate kiss he'd imagined them sharing after months apart. This kiss was hard, angry...merciless. He wanted to bruise her lips like she'd bruised his heart by forcing this distance. He knew he should stop the madness, should step away, but then she kissed him back with the same fervor, a moan bubbling up from her throat, and he was lost. His lips left her mouth and kissed her cheeks, her chin, her neck, up to her ears, and down to the exposed skin of her chest. He let her hands go and wrapped his around her waist, pulling her against him fully, and she moaned again. His lips met hers, and she opened for him, tangling her tongue with his. Her hands clasped in his hair, holding him in place, and she bit his lip. He knew it would be bruised in the morning, and he couldn't wait.

Kevin's voice calling his name down the stairs broke through the fog that had enveloped them. When they separated, they were both panting.

"Are you down here?"

"Yeah. I came down and found Shar had gotten stuck in the bathroom. We just got the door open."

He said that last part loud enough, so anyone else listening would hear the excuse. There was no way Kevin was going to buy it, though.

"Oh shit. Sorry, Shar," Kevin said, also raising his voice nearly as high as his brows. "I should have warned you we need to get that lock fixed."

Kevin took a deep breath, turned and went back upstairs without a word.

"You're right," Shar said when his footsteps were no longer on the stairs.

"About?"

"Avoidance was a good idea." She turned and followed Kevin upstairs.

Mack took a minute to compose himself before he, too, climbed the stairs unsure what just happened or what it meant.

"Absolutely not!" Mack roared, banging his fist on the table.

Everyone around the room looked at each other.

"C'mon, Mack," Kevin responded, his voice even.

"No! Kevin, just no."

"Shar is a professional," Jacques offered, as if that would assuage the situation.

"Do you think I don't fucking know that?" Mack asked, his tone resolute. She's been nothing but professional since we hired her. She's been an absolute rockstar. I am still not okay with that guy putting his hands all over her and pulling her into his lap."

"He, too, has been nothing but professional at every shoot we've done this past year."

Mack stared daggers into their videographer. He didn't give two shits about that guy's supposed professionalism when he'd tried to seduce Shar on their way out here to sign contracts and has likely been biding his time to get a chance with her once they no longer work together.

"You know, there's irony in your behavior right now," Kevin said, his face the picture of exhaustion. He'd been growing wearier as Tabitha got closer to delivering the baby.

Mack glared. "We are so close to the end of this. I will not sit back and watch this happen the way it's written in the script."

"Then don't! You've avoided damn near every shoot thus far."

"Don't push me, Kevin. Not now, after all this time, and not about this. You knew I wasn't going to be okay with any of this, and that's why you didn't want to show me back when we first talked about this final campaign. That's fucked up." His voice softened at the end, as the reality of his friend's betrayal set in, but he couldn't remove the venom.

"Sorry, gentlemen. Normally, we would not air our disagreements in front of witnesses, but my partner here is right. I did keep these details from him because I knew he would fly off the handle like he's doing now. I had hoped he'd just decide not to show up today." Kevin's gaze never left Mack's, even though he addressed his words to other men in the room.

"The fact you would put profits over our friendship..." Mack shook his head incredulously. It was unfathomable.

"I did it because I'm your friend, you fucking idiot!" Kevin yelled for the first time since the four of them had closed themselves in what might as well be called the war room. "She will hate you if you do not let her finish out the contract. Then what would all this whining and pining have been for?"

The two onlookers passed glances between themselves, and Mack thought to send them away, but they needed to know what the plan for the day was going to be.

"He wants to fuck her, Kev. It's not right to put her in the situation to be on his lap for a marketing ad."

"So do you," his friend returned without remorse.

Mouths dropped around the room, Mack's included. He knew he had pissed Kevin off, pushed too far without any solution to the problem he was creating, but he didn't think he'd be called out that directly in front of others. If they had been alone, he'd have retorted with a quick, and the feelings are mutual, but he wouldn't do that to Shar, not in front of professionals she'd likely work with again later. Rather than address his friend, he turned to the others.

"I'm sorry you two had to be here for all of this, truly. Long story short, there is history between Shar and I that goes back before she started working for Velocity. There has been nothing between us since, but that doesn't mean I don't still want to make sure she is safe and treated fairly in the work she does for us."

Thankfully, both men gave him a wide-eyed look of understanding. They accepted his explanation and smiled.

Jacques spoke, "I don't think any of us are surprised to hear that Henri has a thing for Shar. They had strong chemistry when they worked together before. She is a stunning woman, and there is something alluring about her. I'm sure she would not appreciate being put into a compromising position if she knew his intentions and was uninterested. She's a professional but not a pushover."

"No, Shar is anything but a pushover," Mack agreed.

"Would you two mind giving us a minute? Then we will have the plan for the day."

Kevin still had not said another word, and he remained silent until the others left the room. In fact, he hadn't looked at Mack since his scathing comment.

"Kevin, I know you are frustrated with me. Hell, I am frustrated with me. But I'm right about this. Her agent, Jerry, is the one who told me about Henri's attempted seduction the night before they signed the contracts with us. It would be improper and intentionally harmful to put her in that situation on his lap, even if there wasn't something between us."

Kevin finally looked up at him, and Mack saw the remorse in his eyes. He gave his friend a tight-lipped smile.

"I'm sorry," Kevin said. "I have no excuse for putting your business out there like that, even in anger."

"This," Mack said, gesturing around the table at all of the papers and scripts he had strewn about in his anger, "will not break us, my friend."

"Can you at least admit that some of your response is jealousy? That some of it is your inability to accept she would be in someone else's arms, even for little more than a moment?"

"Of course, it is. I can't deny that. I am drowning in emotions for this woman, and all I've been able to get from her is stolen moments she later regrets for nearly a year. The idea of someone else feeling her heat on his lap kills me in a way I can't even describe."

"Then you do the shoot?"

"What?"

"You do it. You be her co-star."

"What about Henri and his crew stationed out there?"

"I'll make up something. Look, I told you that if you were able to control yourself, allowing her to work for the year, I would help you get a chance with her. Why not today? This shoot fulfills her contract."

"Will my stepping in make anyone look at her differently? I also don't want to ruin Henri's career. I don't want him touching her, but I have nothing against the man."

"I will send them home before the shoot starts, before you even come outside. It's not like you've never been in any of the company's ads before. You were once the face of Velocity," Kevin said with a smirk.

"I need the entire place vacated silently and as quickly as possible once the final scene is set. We don't need the lap pictures for cell phone ads. What we get before that will be enough. Can you make that happen?"

"Yeah boss," Kevin said, punching Mack in the arm. Mack shook his offered hand and hugged him.

They quickly explained the plan to the men waiting outside, and then Kevin sent in two stylists to get Mack ready.

CHAPTER 32
SHAR

S
har sat with her co-star. They were already thirty minutes behind schedule for this video and photo shoot while waiting for some last-minute meeting to end. The contract was nearly completed, and she was ready to go. It had been a long week of shoots, an excruciatingly long week back at the beach again without seeing Mack.

According to the gossip mill that was a week-long shoot, Mack was usually more hands on with things like this. She scoffed. He was obviously avoiding her after he'd accosted her in Kevin and Tabitha's basement, which told her all she needed to know about his feelings. Good, she thought. It'd be easier to put this whole situation behind her completely if she never saw him again. She'd also be sure to tell Jerry that she couldn't work for Velocity again once it was all over. She wouldn't get her hopes up over this man again.

Finally, Kevin, Jacques, and the company's personal videographer walked onto the set. Kevin was an awkward middle-aged man when things were going well, but he was downright disheveled when they were not. As the trio approached the center of everyone waiting, he shifted between his two feet, and alternated shoving his hands in his pocket and rubbing his palms on his hips. The other two looked resigned and ready to work, gesturing commands to their assistants without a word.

"There have been some last-minute changes for today's shoot," Kevin shouted, so everyone could hear him. "This will be the last shoot of the contract. Everyone will still be paid their full amounts, even if they're not needed today. Ms. Maxwell's team will remain. No one else is needed." As rumbles of discontent and concern spread from the other teams, Kevin spoke again. "Remember, everyone will get paid for the day regardless of your participation in this last shoot."

Shar walked over to Jacques and asked what was happening. Her friend, who was usually cheery and open simply shrugged and continued to unpack his lenses. The stylist came to take her back to hair and makeup for touchups. She'd not done anything for the last hour, but if they wanted to fluff her hair and powder her nose again, so be it.

"I hear Mr. Mackenzie is inside getting prepped for today's shoot." One of the assistants said to another.

Shar tried to lean closer to the voices from her chair, but it was hard with the stylist playing in her hair. Their voices modulated up and down, and she could hardly hear them. When she couldn't hold back her questions any longer, she stepped out of her chair in their direction.

"Did you say that Sloan Mackenzie is stepping into today's shoot, as in he will be on camera?"

"Yeah, they say he did this from time to time previously. That's why he showed up in so many of the ads from last year," one of them answered.

The other chimed in, "Makes sense though. He's just as dreamy as that model they've had here."

Shar walked away from them. Mack was going to be in this shoot, on camera, with her. She wasn't prepared for the slew of emotions crashing through her chest. Excitement at seeing him again. Fear at seeing him again. Confusion. Why would he choose to come today of all days? Why not just wait for the next ad campaign? He'd probably be happier not seeing her again anyway.

"Ms. Maxwell, you're needed on set."

Shar took a deep steadying breath. "I am Sharlene Maxwell, and I can do this." Plastering a serene smile on her face, she walked over to the Raven that was parked in the middle of the set. The car was sleek, black, and screamed luxury. They wouldn't let anyone near it earlier, but she heard it had the softest leather seats on the market. She was afraid to look up the price.

"Shar, you and Sloan," Jacques started before he was interrupted.

"Call me Mack." Shar's eyes rolled.

"You and Mack," he began again. "You will stand here outside of the car with Mack's back toward the front of the car. Mack, you'll be looking down at her. Your hand will be in your pants pocket, and your jacket will be pulled back to display the phone in its holder on your hip. Shar, you will be facing Mack with your arms up around his neck. Your front hand will hold the cell phone against his back. You will be looking up at him."

Shar hated the way they made her feel like a rag doll during these shoots, just as much as she loved her job. Being placed up against Mack, though, made to touch his body and wrap her hands around his neck...it was all so unnerving. Her body tingled wherever it touched his. It was hard being mad at him and hurt, and yet completely...

"That's it," Jacques yelled. "You haven't seen each other in a while, and he arrives to pick you up for your date."

She looked up into Mack's eyes. She expected them to be cold and empty, much like her co-star's had been on each shoot. Going through the motions but aloof. Mack's, on the other hand, were warm. There was such longing in them that her mouth opened in a silent gasp.

"Yes, Shar, that's the expression. Perfect."

"Perfect," Mack repeated, and she stepped out of his arms, immediately regretting the move when goosebumps formed on her arms. How was it he stole her heat every damn time?

The videographer, whose name she could not remember even after an entire week on the set, stepped forward as the lead for this scene. This time, they were both inside the car, supposedly on the way to their date. Whoever said the leather was soft did not do it justice. She could have slept on this cloud. In this scene, Mack had to press talk on the car's control while his phone sat in the raised cup holder. Shar was on her phone scrolling. They would superimpose a social media app on it later. Then Mack would hang up the call and reach over to run his hand up Shar's thigh.

She was glad to have her phone in her hand as a prop. It allowed her to pretend to respond to something she saw online because her body went haywire as soon as his skin touched hers. Her first thought was how much the cleaning bill would cost when she came all over the seat. Her second thought was how little she cared. When Mack turned to her and said, "Look at me," she knew it was all over. Her pussy clenched, and her clit ached for him.

"Cut. Great job you two. You have great chemistry on camera."

Mack looked at her and winked. She sat as stoically as possible. Remaining professional was getting harder and harder with each change.

"For this last scene, there will be much more movement. It is a very intimate scene at the end of the night. You're driving her home, Mack, and you keep looking at her thighs. You've missed her like crazy, and dinner wasn't enough. You pull over into an empty parking lot and pull her onto your lap."

Shar gasped. Unlike with TV shows and movies, she never got a full rundown of each scene ahead of time. Plans changed all the time, so she usually found out on set, unless nudity was involved. That type of scene was always negotiated as part of the contract and never sprung on her at the last minute.

"Is everything alright, Ms. Maxwell?" the videographer asked.

"Yes." Her voice cracked, and she asked for some water. After taking a drink, she tried again. "Yes, everything is fine. I was just trying to figure out the logistics of getting over there across this console."

"Don't worry," Mack interjected before anyone else could say anything, "I'll make sure you don't get hurt."

There go those conflicted emotions again. He had hurt her already. Yet, her insides warmed thinking about him not only holding her up as she transitioned over there but then her straddling his lap. My god, she was going to have a full-blown orgasm and break down in tears at the same time in the middle of a photo shoot.

"Everyone ready?" The videographer asked them before stepping back and lifting his camera. Jacques would get still photos from her side of the car. Both she and Mack nodded.

Shar again had her phone in her hand and was scrolling, trying to give a good view of the phone for the cameras. She could feel Mack's eyes on her, but she didn't want to look his way.

"I've missed you," he said, and her breath caught.

She knew it was part of the scene but still, his words snatched her heart up. When he reached over and ran his hand up her thigh, under her dress, her heartbeat rose until she was near panting. He took the phone from her hand and threw it in the backseat. Kissing the inside of her wrist, he used his freehand to turn her chin in his direction. "Come here." And she did. Somehow, he lifted her from her side of the car to his lap faster than she could think of where to put her legs.

With her legs on either side of him, her sex pressed against his erection, and fuck was he erect. "Shar." Her name was a plea on his lips, and his eyes bore into hers. "I'm fucking sorry.

Initially, I didn't know, and afterward, I didn't know what to do. You don't have to believe me. Hell, I wouldn't believe me because I should have known. Maybe I just didn't want to do the math. These past months have been shit, absolute shit, and I can't do this anymore."

"Stop." she said on a whisper, tears forming in her eyes. "If I start crying, my makeup will run, and all this work will be ruined. The photos, the videos, everything. I don't want everyone to see me cry."

"Hey, there's nobody here, pretty. Just me and you, at least it better be just me and you."

She froze for a second and then looked around. The set was empty, and most of the lights were off. "When? How? Why?" She looked to him for explanation. It was so hard to remain still and focused on the conversation while straddling him, but she needed to know. To his credit, once she was over there, he'd kept his hands off her.

He ran his hand through his hair. "Every day, I would get the plans for the photo or video shoot. I knew you didn't really want to see me, and I intended to follow your professional wishes." She watched him carefully, trying to find any clue that he might be lying. "Last night, I got today's plan, and this scene, as described was in there. I couldn't. Fuck, Shar, I couldn't fucking sleep imagining you straddling that guy's lap with his hands on your hips. Not for my damn ad campaign. Not when I'd have to look at it and show it in board meetings. Not when I couldn't touch you."

"Mack." Her voice was much firmer this time, and he stopped talking, a question in his gaze. "I need you to touch me."

That was all it took. His hands were all over her. In her hair, pulling her mouth to his. Under her dress, grabbing her ass and rocking her hips back and forth along the length of his cock. Sliding the straps of her dress off her shoulders, so he could suck on her nipples.

"Mack, please."

"Please what, pretty. Anything you want."

"Inside of me now."

He reached between them, and she leaned back, accidentally blowing the horn. They both jumped, and he laughed. His laughter stopped when he rubbed against her wet panties. Looking into her eyes, he bit his lip. It was her turn to laugh.

"Not this time. You can taste me later. Right now, I need you to fill me. I've been so empty."

"Fuck, that is the sexiest thing anyone has ever said to me."

Once his cock was free of his pants, he yanked her panties to the side, and slid her down on shaft. She was so wet, he slid in all the way without obstruction.

"Holy fuck, you feel so good, Mack."

"This is your show, babydoll. Take what you need. I'm all yours."

The earnestness in his voice drove her, pushed her to ride his cock like her life depended on it. As she got closer, he spurred her on, thrusting up every time she descended. Her release built, her walls tightening around him. He reached between them and rubbed her clit, pushing her over the edge, so he could fall with her.

"You're so damn good, Shar. Perfect. You're fucking perfect." With each word, he kissed her face and her head, hugging her close. "I don't want you to leave because the contract is over. I want you to stay with me. Let's try this again. If it works, great. If it doesn't, it won't be because we didn't try to get it right."

Shar didn't even have to think about it. She had no desire to be without him. He was everything she needed, and she hadn't deprived herself for all this time just to walk away stubbornly when he wanted the same thing she did...a chance.

CHAPTER 33
MACK

Mack woke to the smell of bacon. Opening his eyes, he looked around at his bedroom. Clothes were strewn about the floor, his blanket was completely off the bed, the door was wide open. He closed his eyes again, trying to make sense of what was happening. His mind conjured Shar, as it had every night and every morning for months. He felt the weight of her atop him and the smell of her hair wrapped around his senses. He could taste her kiss. He groaned. When would this nightmare be over? And why the fuck did his house smell like bacon?

Getting up from the bed, he grabbed a pair of shorts and slipped them on. He needed to clean up this pigsty of a room. Kevin was right, he was losing his grip and failing to take care of himself. He grabbed the blanket from the floor and tossed it back onto the bed. There were only two people who had keys to his house, so maybe Kevin had come by to make sure he hadn't completely given up on reality after their fight.

"Dude, it was nice of you to come check on me, but you didn't have to make..." he froze in the doorway that led to the open kitchen.

"Good morning, sunshine." Her voice was lilting and happy.

She was wearing one of his t-shirts that barely covered her ass, leaving those beautiful, thick thighs fully exposed. Her hair cascaded down her back in tousled waves. He stood staring at her, unable to say anything or move. After a few moments that seemed like forever, he walked toward her. She was cracking eggs into a pan, having taken the bacon out. He reached his hands around her waist and pulled her against him. She giggled and slapped his hands that had now locked at her belly button.

"You're really here," he said, more of a question than a statement.

"Of course I'm here, silly. You drove us back here yesterday. Where would I go?"

She tried to take a step forward, but he wasn't ready to release her.

"I'm not dreaming?"

With his arms pressed so tightly against her core, he felt her stiffen slightly, pausing. Then she sat the spatula on the counter and spun around in his arms to look up at him. She stared into his eyes and pressed her palms to his cheeks, first one and then the other. When she smiled, he relaxed into her. She was there, really there.

"We must be sharing the same dream then," she said, grabbing his ears and pulling his face down to hers.

He met her lips, softly, tentative at first. Within moments, passion and desire took over, and he deepened the kiss. His tongue plunged into her open mouth and danced with hers. She moaned, and he tasted bacon on her breath. His hands slid down from her waist to grasp her ass, and he pulled her hard against his growing erection. She moaned again, and he envisioned her on his lap in a car. Then he saw her leaned over the counter, his face smothered in her ass. They'd moved from the kitchen to the bedroom, where they'd gone from the couch to the bed to the floor and back again. He groaned at the clothing between them and began pulling the shirt up to expose all of her. She grabbed his hand to stop him, and he couldn't hide his disappointment.

"I'm about to burn the eggs already, and I'm hungry. Feed me first, and you can have whatever you want," she said while turning back to the stove to flip the eggs that would no longer be a perfect over medium."

"Right, sorry. It was the smell of bacon that woke me, but then you brought me to life."

She smiled over her shoulder at him. "Here," she said, passing the loaf of bread behind her. "Make us some toast."

"Yes, ma'am."

"Don't ma'am me, old man."

"I'm not the one who needed to eat before performing."

"That's because you weren't the one on the menu all night."

He popped the bread in the toaster with a smirk. Fuck, he'd missed her. They'd only had one weekend together, but this banter and play between them had been enough to push him over. Stopping his train of thought, he considered her from behind. She was a glorious sight, though it wasn't just her attractive curves and overall softness. He'd have still wanted her without those. It was these quiet moments, the ones they spent in random domesticity, like making breakfast, that captivated him. He had never had this with anyone else, never even pictured the possibility. Now, he wanted all these moments with her.

She set the plates on the counter just as the toaster popped. He joined her, realizing he was starving as soon as he took the first bite.

"Looks like you were actually hungry for food too, huh?"

The smirk on her face made him chuckle. "Yeah. I guess I was." He stood and began massaging her shoulders. When she popped the last bite of toast in her mouth, he leaned down to her ear. "And now, I'm hungry for something else."

"Sir?" Her voice was quiet, but her eyes were shining with excitement.

"That 'sir' makes me what to take you over my knee."

Watching her body react was almost as intoxicating as her taste. Here face flushed at his words, and her nipples hardened, pressing against the cotton fabric. He had no doubt her pussy was wet too.

"Your body is telling on you, Pretty. You want me to spank you."

She took in a shuddering breath and looked up at him, pupils dilated. He smiled, showing his teeth and held out a hand to her. She took it and hopped off the barstool. Rather than lead her back into the messy bedroom, he led her downstairs and through the game room to the theater they'd enjoyed last time she was here. He sat on one of the lower couches rather than choose a mattress.

"Take off that shirt," he demanded.

Without hesitation, she complied, immediately naked to his gaze. He took her in from head to toe, and she stood there allowing his enjoyment of her body.

"Good girl. Now, come kneel on this cushion."

He pointed to the one right next to him. As soon as she was on her knees, he grabbed her shoulders and pulled her across his lap, folding her at the hips, so that her ass stayed in the air. He rubbed his hand over the exposed flesh of her thighs and buttocks, and he slid his hand between her legs to verify her arousal.

"Always so wet for me, Pretty," he said with a low voice, running his fingers over his tongue to savor her taste.

She wiggled at his touch, and he wrapped his hand around her thighs to hold her in place. She still squirmed, and he gave a sharp, unannounced slap to her right butt cheek. She squealed and writhed against him.

"Hold still, or I will add more. That one was just to get your attention."

She groaned, but she held her body more still than she had been. He rubbed the spot he had slapped to ease the sting.

"I wonder how long it will take before you're begging me to make you come. You're already soaked, and your response to that first slap was more arousal than pain. You might just enjoy this more than I will."

He slapped her left cheek, and her surprised squeal turned to a moan. He repeated the gesture, slapping one side and then the other. Soon, her ass was pink on both sides from his hand. His cock screamed for release from the shorts holding him in place, but Mack focused on Shar. She had not yet begged for more. He slapped her upper thigh, catching the sensitive spot between her legs with his fingertips. She drew in a quick breath.

CHAPTER 34

SHAR

Shar wanted to talk about the feelings between them and what they hoped to get from this thing they were finally allowing to happen, but his hands on her body was the sweetest distraction. Though he had made it clear that he planned to spank her, she wasn't ready for the sting. She also wasn't ready for how wet it made her. She'd never let anyone dominate her before Mack, and she still didn't understand how he'd gotten that upper hand. How had he known what her body would respond to more than she did?

Thwack!

She sucked in a deep breath, holding it until the pain subsided when his hand rubbed the same spot. When he caught her pussy lips in the next slap, her body gushed. "Fuck, Mack." This time her cry came out as a moan rather than surprised pain. When he rubbed the spot, she ground herself against his hand, and he laughed.

"Which do you like more, Pretty? The punishment or the reward?"

"Yes," was all she could manage as he swatted her bottom again before quickly repeating his slap on the inside of her other thigh, catching her lips again. She moaned, deep and guttural. Fuck, he was going to make her come like this. Shock ran through her body on a shiver.

"Your ass is so nice and pink right now. Just beautiful." He leaned down and pressed his lips to each of her cheeks while he rubbed the skin around the sensitive spot between her thighs.

"Mack," she cried in frustration. He was touching everywhere except where she needed his touch.

"Tell me what you need." He continued his soothing rubs, which had her breaths ragged with need.

"Rub my clit. Finger me. Eat my ass. Something to make me come. I can't take that teasing." Her words came out raspy with arousal.

"Such a needy minx," he said on a laugh still skirting around the outside of her pussy.

When he took both hands and began massaging her ass so that her cheeks and lips spread on each circular motion, she groaned. She tried to slip her hand between her legs, and he stopped her by pulling her hand up behind her back to rest on the top of her ass, and then he gave her three quick slaps.

"Did I give you permission to touch yourself, Pretty?"

"Mack?" This time, she whimpered his name. She wasn't expecting those slaps, and they were harder than his previous ones. She also wasn't expecting to become even more aroused from them. "I need...I need more."

"More?" His voice lifted, and she knew he was smirking, though she couldn't see his face.

"Please."

He pulled her torso up, letting her arm flop free, and she looked him in the eye. Desire was so obvious that she gasped at the dark look he gave her. She wanted to lean in and kiss him, but she was afraid he'd go back to spanking her, and she needed more. He flipped her around, so her legs straddled him, and she couldn't stop from rubbing herself against him, trying to find her release. He shook his head, and she froze with another whimper.

"You're so fucking beautiful, Shar."

There was a shift in his emotions, and the look in his eyes intensified, though not with lust. This was different. She watched, as his expressions went haywire, until he centered on something akin to pain. Unsure what was happening or what to do, she put her hands on either side of his face and leaned her forehead against his. He wrapped his arms around her, holding her tightly against him while he took deep, centering breaths.

"This would be so much easier if it was just about the sex." He shook his head against her hands but did not pull away.

"Sex is easy." She ran her fingers through his hair, massaging his scalp while he worked through whatever had taken a hold of him.

"Sex is easy," he repeated, "or at least it used to be." He loosened his grip and pulled back slightly to look at her. She held his gaze.

"This hasn't been any easier for me, Mack. I promise you. I've been losing my mind. You were supposed to be a fun fling in California, like all the other fun flings I've had over the years while traveling for work." His eyes widened, and she shrugged. "Like you said, sex is easy, but nothing about you has been easy."

"My first intention when you sent me that napkin was to break that control you thought you had and make you beg me for it back."

She raised a brow at that confession and then smiled at the memory of his commands. "You were successful that night."

"Yea," he said with a smirk, "except I didn't realize how easy packing up to leave and go on with life would be for you after the night we'd had."

Laughing, she said, "You do remember that you left first, right?"

With one arm round her waist, he lifted her off him and

slapped her ass. Her mouth dropped open in surprise, and he shrugged. "That's what you get for being cheeky."

"Cheeky, huh? So, you slap my cheeks?" She pursed her lips and shook her head. He laughed harder before sobering again.

"I didn't want to leave. Everything in me told me to stay, but I had a meeting first thing in the morning. It was a meeting I didn't want to do, wasn't fully prepared for, and I arrived late. The entire day was fucked, and all I could think throughout the morning was getting back to the hotel, riding the waves, and then finding you to ride your waves again."

"Does it make you feel any better to know that you were on my mind the entire day too? I went to my photo shoot and then found out I had to spend an extra night in Cali before flying out here. I was pissed that I had already checked out of the hotel."

He gave her a sheepish grin. "Maybe it makes me feel a little better, but no."

"Too used to getting what you want, Mr. CEO?"

His laugh was dark. "I never expect to get what I want without having to give a little, whether it's pleasure, payment, or time. Some lessons we learn young and never forget."

"You can say that again." She tried to keep ancient memories from surfacing. His words brought up visions of her mother, and she wasn't quite ready to share that part of her with him. "So what is it that you want, Mack, and what are you willing to give for it?"

He wound his arms tightly around her again and buried his nose in her hair. "I want these authentic moments with you. I want to hear your laughter. I want to wake up to your smile. I want to bury myself in you and have you scream my name. Mostly, I want to feel without the fear that it will all just go away in a moment."

Tears welled in Shar's eyes at his words and the vulnerability he showed in sharing them. She couldn't bring herself to look up at him because she knew they would start streaming down her face.

"Oh, and I'm willing to give whatever it takes. I already know the alternative isn't worth being stingy."

Shar laughed, and it turned into a sniffle. Her emotions were roiling. She leaned close and snuggled her face into his neck. When she'd finally gotten control of herself again, she pulled back and kissed his cheek and then his temple.

"I don't know how to do this thing you're asking. I have no experience with happy endings, except the ones that have me screaming your name." Sadness passed over his face, his eyes cast downward. "But," she continued before the emotion could take hold completely, "I'm willing to try if you are willing to be patient with me."

He looked deep into her eyes, like he was trying to read her thoughts. Then he put his hands to her cheeks like she had done to him earlier, and he kissed her lightly, slowly, taking his time. "We survived this year. I believe we can handle whatever else comes up." This time, when he pressed his lips to hers, she poured her emotions into the kiss, pushing it deeper, giving herself to him, and he took it all.

EPILOGUE
SHAR

Shar was disappointed Mack couldn't come to pick her up from the airport. She'd missed him desperately while she was home packing her house and putting it on the market. The past two weeks since they'd decided to move in together formally felt longer than the months they'd spent actively avoiding each other earlier that year. Something about committing to each other made the separation harder. She collected the one suitcase she'd brought with her and looked for Velocity's driver. Rather than finding Fred waiting at the door, she saw Tabitha waddling down the sidewalk. She rushed out to greet her.

"What are you doing here? Look at you. You should be home resting."

"Not you too," Tabitha complained. "If I rest any more, I might as well be in a fucking coma. I'm having a baby not dying of pneumonia for fuck's sake."

Shar laughed at her friend. "Two fucks in one sentence? I think that's a record for you," she teased.

"Oh, you've not heard anything yet. My damn husband won't stop treating me like a porcelain doll that could break if the air blows in the wrong direction. I need this child to come on out into the world, just so he can focus on something else besides me."

"Okay, momma," Shar said, wrapping her arm around Tabitha's and leading her to the door. "You can tell me all about it in the car. Where'd you park?"

"That's another fucking thing," her friend screeched, "he took my goddamn keys away, saying that driving was too dangerous now. So, I have to rely on Fred to take me everywhere. You know he's not great company." Her indignation shifted to frustration and then to excitement as she finished with, "I'm so glad you're home! I've missed you."

Shar squeezed the other woman around her back and shoulders because she could not have reached around her belly. Tabitha looked like she was ready to pop any day. She could barely pull herself up into the SUV, not waiting for Fred to put down the step stool after he'd put Shar's suitcase in the back.

"Thank you, Fred," Shar said. Tabitha just glared at the step in his hands. He nodded to her in acknowledgement and helped Tabitha up into the back seat.

The women fell into easy conversation around the move and the baby. Tabitha asked if she had any photo shoots coming up, and Shar shook her head.

"I'm taking some time off to get settled here, but maybe after the wedding, I'll have Jerry find me some things."

Tabitha rubbed her abdomen silently, though her mouth was open. When her eyes widened in surprise, Shar reached out a hand.

"Are you okay, Tabs?"

Shaking her head, Tabitha whispered, "Either I just peed myself or my water broke."

"Oh shit! Fred. Fred!"

Shar's breaths were coming quickly, almost more quickly than Tabitha's, and the car's lack of air felt stuffy. Fred turned to look at her through the rearview.

"Hospital," was all she could manage to say.

"Ms. Maxwell?"

"We're about to have a baby in the backseat, so I think we should head to the hospital."

Fred's eyes went wide, and he flipped on the blinker, yelling at people to move out of the way and let him get off the exit.

"That's the most animated I have ever seen him," Tabitha said under her breath, and Shar laughed despite her rising panic.

Taking out her phone, she sent a text to Mack.

> Is Kevin with you?

> Mack: Is everything okay?

> Is he with you?

> Mack: Yes, we're in the middle of a virtual call with international investors.

> Apologize and get in the car.

> Mack: Shar?

"What hospital are we going to?" Shar asked Fred.

"Wrighton General is the one Mr. Dulaney instructed me to take her."

> We'll be at Wrighton General. We're about to have a baby.

> Well, not us.

> Them.

> Tabitha. Her water just broke in the car.

> Mack: On the way!

"Mack is going to bring your husband to the hospital," she told Tabitha.

Still rubbing her abdomen, Tabitha responded with an exhausted laugh, "Does he have to?"

"You'd be pissed if he didn't, now just lean back and rest. We'll be there soon enough."

Though she'd said the words, Shar wasn't sure she believed them herself. She had no idea what it was like to have a baby or how long it took after a woman's water broke for the baby to come out. She couldn't deliver a baby. She looked toward Fred who was still frantically gesturing for other drivers to get out the way. The way he was freaking out did not bode well for him knowing how to deliver a baby either. Rather than ask Fred how much longer they'd be, she pulled it up on her GPS. They were still fifteen minutes away. Leave it to Kevin to have planned out the exact hospital regardless of where his wife happened to be in the city. She rolled her eyes and let out a huff. When Tabitha opened her eyes in Shar's direction, she simply shook her head.

"Ignore me," Shar said, patting her friend's arm and then closing her own eyes to take some calming breaths.

Thanks to traffic, the drive took twenty-five minutes, and Kevin came running down the hall as they wheeled Tabitha up to labor and delivery. He didn't even acknowledge Shar's presence, all his attention focused on his wife. Before the nurse could get her in the elevator, Kevin was on his knees in tears apologizing for not being there. Shar shook her head. That poor guy is going to lose his mind if this baby is a girl. Her thoughts wandered to all the possibilities when strong arms wrapped around her from behind. Instantly, her nerves calmed, and the trembling that had begun in the car stopped.

"I've missed you," he said against her hair. "I'm sorry I wasn't there to pick you up."

Shar turned in his arms to look up at him. "I've missed you. I'm just glad Tabitha came with Fred and wasn't home alone when this happened. I'd be like Kevin, down on my knees begging forgiveness."

"There's only one reason for you to be on your knees," he said with a lascivious smile, "but that can wait until we get home."

She smirked before lifting on her toes to kiss his lips. The same nurse who had taken Tabitha upstairs interrupted their greeting and directed them to the appropriate waiting room where they spent the rest of the morning and half of the afternoon.

Hair and makeup took far longer than Shar expected. Who knew how many pins had been used or how much hairspray? If the veil hadn't come with a comb to hold it in place, the lace would have simply remained glued in place anyway. The dress fit perfectly. It was elegant and hugged the curves. A knock at the door had her heart jumping.

"Don't come in," Shar yelled through the closed door.

"It's time," Mack said just loud enough that she could hear him.

She smiled unable to wait until she was back in his arms. One quick trip down the aisle would do it. When they were sure no one was in the hallway who shouldn't be, the entourage walked out of the building and onto the boardwalk.

The wedding would happen on Mack's new yacht, but first the couple would have to pass through everyone who'd come with well wishes. Music started as soon as they'd stepped from concrete to the wooden planks along the harbor. The song was not the wedding march, as nothing about this wedding was traditional, but it held plenty of memories.

Shar grasped the bouquet tight, not wanting it to slip

from her sweaty hands while she climbed onto the yacht. She looked up to see Mack staring down at her from the upper deck where a wooden arch had been erected. Kevin was up there too. When Shar crested the top of the stairs, Mack reached out a hand to her. She took it with a smile, and he kissed her cheek before directing her to the opposite side of the arch near where he stood in the middle. He looked delectable in his perfectly tailored Italian suit, the only thing he'd bought during their outing in Turin while Tabitha and she had been shopping for lingerie.

The music stopped, and the gathering went silent. Shar took a moment to look around at everyone. So many of her favorite people were here. Tabitha was by her side, holding the huge bridal bouquet, and Kevin was on the other side of the arch holding their one-month-old daughter, Kassandra, or Kassie for short. Then she looked at the man she loved, because she knew it was love she felt for him, and her heart soared. He picked up the book that sat on the table next to him and began to read from the script the happy couple had chosen when they asked him to officiate their wedding, now that he was the captain of his own boat.

"Friends and family, we are gathered here today to support Charles and Janet on their first day as husband and wife. Charlie and Janet, as you go into married life, remember the reason you've chosen to become partners in this life. Let that be the reason you wake up with a smile, get ready with purpose, give your all each day, and rush home to each other's arms. Remember this reason through every sacrifice, every instance of giving, and every bout of laughter. This is the reason you are legally binding yourself to one another, to not bear each joy and each burden alone."

Shar wiped a tear from her eye. She'd been to weddings before, but she'd never focused on the words of the ceremony. Somehow hearing Mack speak of a lifelong partnership to share in the good and the bad made her look at relationships and marriage differently. When Janet and Charlie kissed each other, she cheered aloud, and as soon as the couple walked down the stairs to have their photos taken, she flung herself into Mack's arms.

"That was truly beautiful, my love," she said, wrapping her arms tightly around him.

He stood absolutely still, his arms still down at his sides. She loosened her hold on him and stepped back to see his face. His eyes were a combination of confusion and wariness, while his head tilted to the side.

"What did you say?" he asked quietly.

"I said you did a beautiful job with the ceremony."

"No, after that. At the end."

Shar had to think for a moment. What had she said? Whatever it was had come naturally because she had no clear recollection.

"What did you call me?" he asked her, his voice demanding.

"Oh. 'My love,'" she said.

"Why?"

She nearly laughed at the question, but his expression said that wouldn't be a good idea.

"It's how I feel. I mean, it wasn't something I'd planned to say. Listening to the opening part of the ceremony had me thinking about us, and I realized that at some point, all of the emotions I have felt for you have coalesced into love."

"You love me?"

She let out an anxious chuckle, but her lip quivered slightly. Did he not believe her, or did he not want her to love him? She wasn't asking for him to profess anything back. She looked down at the floor, suddenly self-conscious.

"Please don't pull away from me," he said, his jaw set when she looked up at his face again. "I need to know. Do you love me?"

"Will you be upset if I do?"

He didn't say anything, just watched her. Finally, when she couldn't take the silence anymore, she nodded, reaching up to caress his cheek. "Yes. I love you."

She braced herself for his response, and he leaned into her hand. He opened his mouth as if to say something and then shut it. He repeated these actions three more times before giving her a trembling smile.

"The next wedding will be ours," he said, turning his face into her hand, so he could kiss her palm and then her wrist. Taking her hand, he led her down the stairs. Before she stepped onto the landing, he held her in place, her eyes level with his.

"You are the most beautiful person I've met, Sharlene Maxwell," he said, wrapping his hand around the back of her head. "I didn't realize I was falling in love with you until I was helpless against it. When you made me dance with you in that dive bar in Italy, I was yours, and I have loved you since. My life's mission is to love you forever."

THE END

LEYA LAYNE

Follow Leya all over social media:
https://linktr.ee/LeyaLayneAuthor

See her website for forthcoming releases and trigger/content
warnings:
https://bisabelwrites.com/leyas-content-is-for-18-only/

Coming Soon
November 2024: The Next #HotHallmark Novel [Still
Untitled]

Fall 2024: Falling in Cole County: A Cozy Romance
Anthology

Made in the USA
Columbia, SC
19 August 2024